Corrupted by a Gangsta 3

**Lock Down Publications and
Ca$h Presents**
Corrupted by a Gangsta 3
A Novel by Destiny Skai

Destiny Skai

Lock Down Publications
P.O. Box 870494
Mesquite, Tx 75187

Visit our website
www.lockdownpublications.com

Copyright 2019 by Corrupted by a Gangsta 3

Lock Down Publications
Like our page on Facebook: Lock Down Publications @
www.facebook.com/lockdownpublications.ldp
Cover design and layout by: **Dynasty Cover Me**
Book interior design by: **Shawn Walker**
Edited by: **Kiera Northington**

Stay Connected with Us!

Text **LOCKDOWN** to 22828 to stay up-to-date with new releases, sneak peaks, contests and more…

Submission Guideline.

Submit the first three chapters of your completed manuscript to ldpsubmissions@gmail.com, subject line: Your book's title. The manuscript must be in a .doc file and sent as an attachment. Document should be in Times New Roman, double spaced and in size 12 font. Also, provide your synopsis and full contact information. If sending multiple submissions, they must each be in a separate email.

Have a story but no way to send it electronically? You can still submit to LDP/Ca$h Presents. Send in the first three chapters, written or typed, of your completed manuscript to:

LDP: Submissions Dept
Po Box 870494
Mesquite, Tx 75187

DO NOT send original manuscript. Must be a duplicate.

Provide your synopsis and a cover letter containing your full contact information.

Thanks for considering LDP and Ca$h Presents.

Acknowledgements

The highest praises go to God and my family. My two kings, Torrence and Ethan. The both of you are the reasons mommy goes so hard for you. There is nothing on earth I wouldn't do to make all of your dreams come true.

I would like to thank all of my readers for rocking with me throughout my literary journey and the new ones that have recently come aboard. The love and support is surreal and greatly appreciated. I can honestly say that this is the best series that I have penned to date, with word of mouth it's guaranteed to be a classic and there will be many more in the future. So be on the lookout.

If this is your first time reading my work please go and check out The Fetti Girls and Bride of a Hustla, which is available on Amazon. My first series Bride of a Hustla has a movie, so if you would like to purchase it visit my website: www.thadspot.com. Also, be sure to Subscribe to my YouTube Channel, Destiny Skai.

Upon finishing this book, please be sure to leave a review. They are important to me being that it will help me grow as an author. From the bottom of my heart I appreciate the love and support from all of you.

~Love Destiny

Follow me on all social media sites (FB, IG & Twitter): @Author Destiny Skai and Join my Facebook reading group: Skai's Book Babies.

Recap from Brick...

Coop and I ran out the door in pursuit of her, but she must've run down the stairs or some shit. By the time we made it to the parking lot, she was tossing her bag into the car and climbing inside. He ran up to the driver's side and grabbed the door. I stood there and watched to see if a fight was gone break out before I intervened.

"Danielle, don't do this. I'm not mad about you trying to poison me, so let's go back in the house and talk about this."

"You think I give a fuck because you not mad? No. I don't care and that's why I did it."

Time was flying like a muthafucka, because Zuri was calling my phone already. I answered her call. "Hey, baby. You just landed?"

"Yes."

"How was your flight?"

"It was nice, thanks to my baby getting us first-class seats." That happiness in her voice made my heart melt. All I wanted to do was make her and my daughter happy.

"That's good."

"What you doing? And what is all that noise?"

"Over here in the parking lot at Coop's house, listening to him and his wife argue."

Zuri laughed. "Oh, well, good luck with that."

"I know right, but I'm..." The shouting was elevating by the second and Coop's voice caught my attention.

"Get down, bruh."

The panic in his voice caused my head to swivel in the opposite direction. Coop was running towards me in a fast pace. At first I was confused, but then I finally caught sight of what he was looking at. It was the barrel of a shotgun. My heart rate sped up, being that I was unprepared for what was happening. In slow motion, my phone slipped from my fingertips and hit the concrete. The next thing I heard were multiple gunshots that clapped like thunder.

Chapter 1

Zuri

"Briiick!" I screamed to the top of my lungs. The sound of gunfire was all I heard through the receiver. "Baby, answer me please." The stares from the people at the airport were the least of my worries. I was concerned about my man and father of my unborn child. If they didn't like my outburst, they could kiss my brown ass cheeks.

"What's wrong?" Mehzani dropped her luggage and rushed to my aid.

"I. I. I don't know. I heard gunshots and now he's not responding to me." My hands trembled as I clutched the phone in my hand and the tears began to stream down my face.

Mehzani embraced me in her arms. "Calm down, sis. I'm sure he's okay. Let's not panic right now, because I don't need you upsetting my niece or nephew."

Her response took me by surprise, because I never told her that I was pregnant. So that only meant one thing, Brick told her. It didn't matter though, since I'd planned on telling her sometime during our trip.

"I'm trying, but I don't know if he's okay." My sobs grew louder. "Zani, he's my world and I can't lose him like that."

Mehzani stopped hugging me and grabbed my face in both of her hands. "He's going to be okay and I need you to be strong. I'm here with you, so you don't have to deal with this alone. Okay?"

"Okay." I nodded my head in agreement, but I wasn't sure if I believed that or not.

"Let's go to the beach house, so you can take a shower and relax. Then we will call Brick to see what's going on."

"Okay."

We took an Uber to the Malibu beach house. Instead of me enjoying the ride and sightseeing, my eyes were filled with water, blocking the beautiful view. I kept my phone in my hand just in case Brick called while I was en route. This could not be happening to me. Two losses within two months was entirely too much to bear. My heart just couldn't take it. All I wanted was for all of the pain to go away.

It took roughly forty minutes to get to Malibu. In between the time it took to reach our destination, I constantly dozed on and off for a few minutes at a time. The car came to a stop and I heard the door close, followed by a tap on my shoulder.

"Wake up, sis. We here."

Slowly, I raised my head and I was baffled at the amazing view. With no real sense of urgency, I opened the door and stepped from the vehicle. The car ride had been a long one, so I stretched my arms and legs before grabbing my luggage.

"Do you ladies need any help?" the Uber driver asked.

"No, thank you. We got it." Mehzani answered his question rather quickly and without thought.

"Enjoy your stay," he replied, as he got back inside the car and pulled off.

"Dang, Zani, you dismissed his ass with no hesitation."

"Hell yeah. We don't know his ass. Shit, he might be a kidnapper for all we know."

That mouth of hers made me laugh against my will, but I was grateful. Mehzani and I scrolled gracefully towards the office so we could check in. The sound of the clear, bluish water slapping against the rocks, and the view of the high houses on the hill was absolutely breathtaking. It would be nice to live a home just like it in the future. I could definitely see me and Brick living in a beach house.

The process took no time to complete and we were on our way to start our vacation. Just looking at the outside had me anxious about the way the inside was laid out. The beach house looked more like a condo, by the way it was propped on top of the rocks and boards. Mehzani unlocked the door and stepped to the side so I could walk in first.

As soon as I stepped across the threshold, I was amazed at the set up. The gray and white décor was stunning and a perfect fit for the black and white wall mural, of a woman with bright blue lipstick.

"Damn, this is nice as fuck," Mehzani cheerfully screeched in excitement, while looking at me for approval. "Don't you think so?" She was doing her best to get me to engage. For her sake, I forced a fake smile.

"Yes, it is. My baby really outdid himself." I sat my luggage beside the white leather sofa and sat down.

Brick was on my mind heavily and there was no way I could enjoy myself, without knowing he was okay. He was the sunshine that woke me up in the morning. The reason I could finally leave Daman alone, so I could feel what real love was without the incest. My true reason for living and now with a baby on the way, I couldn't lose him or live without him for that matter.

My phone was in my hand, so I dialed his number. On the first ring, it went to the voicemail and my heart sunk. "Oh my God," I cried. "His phone is going straight to the voicemail."

"Zuri, just relax and remain optimistic. Stop thinking the worst and pray for the best. I'm sure he's okay. Brick looks like he can hold his own."

Tears were streaming down my face and I could feel spit forming at the corners of my mouth. Using my hand, I wiped both sides. "My heart wants to believe that, but my mind is singing a different tune."

Mehzani walked over to the sofa and sat down beside me. Since she was a child, she had always been the nurturing type, so it didn't surprise me when she held me in her arms as I cried. It felt good to have my sister with me to help me through such a critical moment. For the next few minutes, we remained in that same position until the frightening sound of my cellphone interrupted my sobs. It reminded me of an eerie tune from a horror movie, right before someone died.

My hands trembled as I picked up the phone and took a deep breath. It was an unknown number, so that made my nerves worse than they were. If Brick was dead, I might as well commit suicide. I closed my eyes and answered.

"Hello."

"Zuri."

"Brick?" I questioned.

"Yeah, baby, it's me," he replied.

"Oh my God, I thought you were dead." My heart felt a million times stronger.

"I know and that's why I'm calling. I'm okay. My phone broke, so I have to get another one, but I'll call you later."

"Baby, what happened?" My heartbroken cries had quickly turned into tears of joy and I could finally breathe again.

"We'll talk about that later, but in the meantime, enjoy yourself. I'm going to be okay."

"Please be careful. I can't lose you."

"I'm not going anywhere. Don't worry. I love you."

"I love you too."

Brick hung up the phone and I was so relieved. Mehzani was looking at me, smiling. "See, I told you. Now let's go put on our swimsuits and enjoy our trip."

"Okay, let's do it." Finally out of my funk, I was ready to enjoy my vacation. "One two-piece coming up."

"Yassss, fish." Mehzani squatted and made her booty shake. "Let's turn up."

* * *

Brick

Now that I was able to put Zuri's mind at ease, it was time to figure out who the fuck was shooting at me and why. Thankfully, every bullet shot in my direction missed me by inches. I knew that was nothing but the armor of God. The lifestyle I lived was dangerous, but I never forgot about the person responsible for dying for my sins. As I rushed back into the emergency room, I walked to the back where they were keeping Danielle. One of the bullets grazed her thigh, so she wasn't injured too badly. Coop was standing by her bed, holding her hand. I handed him the phone.

"Thanks, bruh. If Zuri calls back, which she shouldn't, let her know I went to get a phone."

"You out?" he asked, with a concerned look on his face.

"Yeah, I gotta handle this shit, man." I nodded in Danielle's direction. "Sis fucked up behind some bullshit."

"Well, I'm going with you. Ain't no way I'm letting you handle shit solo." He leaned down and kissed Danielle on her cheek. "I'll be back soon," Coop assured her.

"Nah, I'm straight. Stay here with your wife. I got this."

"Brick, I'm okay." Danielle was hoarse from the pain medication. Her voice was just above a whisper. "Don't go out there alone, take Coop with you. I would never forgive myself if something happened to you, knowing I let you go alone."

"On the real, sis, I'm good. I'm on my way to get some protection, so it's all good." Then, I turned to my day-one nigga. "I'm going to holla at Hector, but as soon as I'm done, I'll hit you up."

Coop contemplated my answer for a while before G-hugging me. "Make sure you call me."

"Fa'sho." His hold was tight, like he didn't want to release me. It was all love and we didn't share the same blood, but that don't make you family no way. It's all about that loyalty.

"Bruh, you can let go now. Ain't shit gone happen to me." I joked it off, but in the back of my mind, I knew I needed to be careful. There was no telling who the fuck was watching my every move.

Coop let go and exhaled. "Be safe, bruh."

"I will." Then, I left the room.

On my way to Hector, I watched my surroundings like a hawk. At every stop light, I was cautious of every car or truck that pulled alongside me. That muthafucka caught me off-guard once, it wouldn't be a second time. I had too much to live for and I had my Desert Eagle in my lap, ready to clap at anything suspicious. The shit that was blowing me was, how did the muthafucka find me? No one knew where Coop lived and no one followed me.

When I pulled up, the club was packed and security was at the door, so I knew shit was kosher. I put my bitch under the seat and got out the car. The bouncer recognized me off the top.

"What's up, Brick?" We shook hands.

"Shit. Just cooling. Hector in there?" I didn't know, since I just popped up unannounced.

"Yeah. He in the back."

"A'ight, thanks."

"Yeah."

On the inside, bad chicks were walking around in thongs and some were butt-ass naked. They had some colossal asses and itty-bitty waists. The view was amazing as their oily booty's bounced against the neon lights. I couldn't wait for Zuri to get back, because I needed some pussy bad. Just staring at all the banging bodies made my dick jump. *Calm down, my boy,* I told myself because he was ready to smash some shit. Temptation was calling a nigga, but I promised to be faithful to Zuri, so I kept on pushing to the back.

When I stepped into Hector's favorite section of the club, he was sitting between the twins. There were two other females amongst them. They were all smiles and apparently tipsy.

"Whaddup, Hector?" I slapped his hands and sat down across from him.

"Hey, Brick," the twins sang. They asses were lit like a bitch.

"Sup ladies." I nodded my head.

"Enjoying my lovely twins. What's up with you?" he grinned.

"Shit, coolin'."

Hector looked at two of the girls and nodded in my direction. "Keep my man company."

The two Spanish girls stood up, so I immediately checked out the merchandise. They were both wearing gold net bikinis, with what appeared to be diamonds. They were fine as fuck too, with some sexy-ass tattoos around their waists and thighs. Both women sat on opposite sides of me and snuggled under me, leaving no room to breathe.

Temptation was riding me hard as fuck, so I concentrated on my reason for coming and ignored their wandering hands on my chiseled physique. "I need to holla at you in private."

"We can as soon as you loosen up." Hector was doing his best to make me in engage in something I wanted no parts of.

"I'm good." My eyes were trained on him.

Through the speakers, Juvenile's "Back That Azz Up," flooded the club and the girls became rowdy quick. They didn't waste any time dropping low and making them ass cheeks shake like an earthquake in my face. Leaning back, I put my hands in my pockets to make sure I kept them to myself. For a nigga, it was tempting and easy to get caught up, but as a man, I learned to think with the head on my shoulders and not the one dangling between my legs. My heart and conscience wouldn't let me secretly break my girl's heart. I could never fuck another chick and look her in the eyes and lie about being faithful, especially when I gave her grief about having a male friend.

When the song came to an end, I was low-key happy. That meant I no longer had to endure something I wasn't interested in. Hector was having a ball, but it was time to discuss business. I looked at all the ladies and spoke.

"Can y'all give us a moment to talk? Come back in ten minutes." I sat up and folded my hands to let them know I meant business.

They looked at Hector for approval. "It's okay. Go enjoy the crowd for a little bit, but don't get lost." Once he nodded his head, they stood up and left the area.

"What's going on my friend?" He sat up and met my stare to show I had his attention.

"I need some protection in these streets. My team not big enough for what may be coming my way."

"What's going on?"

"A few hours ago, I was shot at by some white dude." I rubbed my face in frustration. "I don't know who the fuck this nigga is or how he found me."

"Were you followed?"

"Nah. I pay attention to all of that and nobody knows where my number-two lives. This shit crazy." I sighed.

"You sure about that?" he questioned me like I was a rookie or some shit.

"Hell, yeah. I ain't new to this shit. Nobody followed me." All that twenty-question shit was nerve-racking.

"If you ain't being followed, all I can say is that maybe it's a tracker on your car. In this business, that's common. I'll have someone check your car."

"And what about the protection?" I asked to make sure he didn't forget my purpose in coming to him in the first place.

"Consider it done. I can arrange to have two of my best men to serve as your bodyguard and in the event that something transpires, just call for backup. In the meantime, be aware of your surroundings and be careful with the work. We can't afford to lose money."

Hector was a solid dude who would always have my loyalty, although I knew his main reason for agreeing was to make sure his investment remained safe. "That's what's up. I appreciate that, man. Real shit. My biggest concern is my lady and…" And, that's when it hit me like a Mayweather punch. The wheels in my head got to turning fast.

"Now that I think of it, about a week ago I spotted a truck across the street from my lady's house. That shit was out the ordinary, because I had never seen it before. I'm almost certain this was the same dude."

"Well, I would suggest she don't stay there until we get a handle on who's behind the hit. You don't want a tragedy of wrong place, wrong time."

"She in Cali right now, but when she get back, I'll make it happen. I'll lay down the whole state about her."

My daughter was a major concern, but he didn't need to know my daughter existed, just in case some shit went down between us. In this game, you could never be too careful. No one would ever be able to use Breanna as leverage.

"Are we done here?" Hector stopped looking at me and scanned the crowd. "I'm ready to party."

"Yeah. I'm headed out."

"Come by tomorrow so we can check the car for any tracking devices. Be careful until then."

"Will do." We shook hands, then I left.

When I got inside the car, I shot Skeet a quick text.

Brick: Tomorrow is initiation day
Skeet: Got it Boss

Once he responded, I put my phone away and made my way to see Breanna. The events from that day had me in my feelings. I could never picture myself away from my daughter forever. Not seeing her graduate high school, college, get married or have kids, is not what I had planned. Those were the things I looked forward to doing. Therefore, I knew I had to make sure I stayed alive while maneuvering in these streets. Laying low was probably in my best interest. My goal was to become the Godfather of Lauderdale, so now I needed to reorder my steps.

Chapter 2

Daman

One day had passed and my nerves were shot as I sat and waited for Rock to call me and let me know what the lick read. All I knew was that his muthafuckin' ass better not put Zuri in the crossfire, because if he did, his ass was a dead man walking. I would forget about us being long-time friends and lay him out. As I laid in the bed, staring up at the top bunk, Zuri's beautiful face popped in my mind. It was crazy how she looked so much like her mother and I knew that's what made me love her the way I did. I'm not a saint by far, and I was a hundred percent sure I was going to hell for the shit I did in my life. On Judgement Day, I had one person to answer to and that was the man up above. No man or woman walking on the planet could frown upon the things I did, or formulate judgement on me. They didn't know me or know the demons I had to battle on a daily basis.

It was never in my plans to love her in that manner. That shit just happened. The fact that she told me she wanted to be normal played in my head constantly and broke my heart every time I thought about it. Deep down, I really wish I could help her with that, but I was so deep in I couldn't let her go. My heart wouldn't allow me to see her happy with another man. I would rather see her mourn the loss of that nigga, instead of living happily ever after without me. Zuri and I were supposed to live happily ever after, until that nigga came along and fucked shit up. Now, he was turning her against me and I didn't like that shit one bit.

My anxiety got the best of me, so I hit up Rock.

"I was just about to call you."

"You handled that?" I asked, cutting straight to the chase.

"It's done."

"A'ight, good looking out. I'll send you something once I get confirmation."

"Yeah."

As I hung up the phone, a wide accomplished smile spread across my lips. All I had to do now was wait on Zuri to call me, crying about the loss of her unborn child's father. That is when I would convince her to have an abortion, so she wouldn't have to be a single mother. She saw how it was growing up without both parents in the home, so that should be an easy task. My fingers were itching to dial her number, but she told me not to call her again. I didn't want her to make good on that threat, so I put the phone underneath my pillow and just laid there.

There was a knock on the door and I was hoping it wasn't Tate. I was not in the mood for her mouth or pussy, so I ignored it. The knocking turned into banging and that pissed me off, because a muthafucka was being mad disrespectful.

"Who the fuck is it?" I shouted.

"Cee, nigga."

"Come in." Cee walked in with his eyes all big and shit. "Fuck you in here doing?"

"Minding my fuckin' business. Y'all won't let a nigga rest." I put my hands behind my head.

"We out of product. When the next shipment coming in?" Cee leaned against the bunk with his eyes trained on me.

"A few days. I'll let you know when I get the confirmation."

"A'ight, 'cause these niggas hounding me and shit."

"They better learn how to wait." I rolled over onto my side. "Close the door on your way out."

Cee walked out and closed the door. Ten seconds later, I was calling Zuri, against her wishes. The phone rang a few times and just when I thought I wasn't getting an answer, the ringing stopped and I saw her beautiful face. The pregnancy glow added to her features in a good way, but I couldn't have that shit. She wasn't wearing her usual smile, but she didn't appear to be sad either. Just that alone made me wonder if she knew about her baby daddy.

Zuri stared at me in silence for a few seconds, before she let out a sigh filled with annoyance. "I thought I told you not to call me anymore?"

I knew she was aggravated with me, but I didn't care. My heart wouldn't let me agree to those terms. "I know you didn't really mean that. Besides, I just wanted to check on you." Shrugging my shoulders, I licked my lips out of habit. It wasn't like I was trying to be inviting or anything like that. "You know, to see how you doing, that's all."

Zuri's attitude towards me was obvious. And although I wasn't near her or in her space physically, I could feel the tension through the phone. "I'm fine, but you knew that already. Instead of checking on me, I have someone that you should be checking on."

"Who?" She had me confused as hell.

Zuri moved the phone and the sight of my baby girl blew me away mentally. It had been years since I last saw Mehzani or talked to her for that matter. She looked the same, just older.

"Your daughter," Zuri simply stated.

"I know who she is. I could never forget her face." It was refreshing to finally see her face after all that time.

That immediately took me back to all the letters and phone calls. I attempted to reach her, but my sister didn't want me to have any contact with my very own flesh and blood.

"Wow! Mehzani. It's really good to see you. I've missed you so much."

"Really?" It was hard to tell her mood because we had been out of touch for so long.

"Yes. Despite what happened in the past and the act I subjected you to, I was never upset with you."

"You didn't have a right to. What you did was wrong and you know it." Mehzani was a bit snappy with her reply. So that let me know she wasn't too happy with seeing my face.

"You're right." I paused and thought about what I would say next. Then, it dawned on me that I owed her an explanation, because she was so young at the time. To make sure she understood me, I gave her complete eye contact.

"Mehzani, you were young when that happened and I owe you an explanation about what you saw." She nodded her head, acknowledging that she was listening. "First, you need to know that I never physically hurt your sister. We shared a special bond that was meant for a man and a woman, instead of father and daughter. In my mind, I didn't see anything wrong with it, because I loved her the same way I did your mother."

Mehzani cut me off. "Do you know for years I thought you didn't love me? All because we didn't do the things you and Zuri did. Auntie told me it was wrong and I should be grateful you never did those things to me, because you brainwashed Zuri. After holding that grudge towards you, I let it go and realized you were a pedophile."

"That's not true," I interjected, not wanting her to label me as a monster. "God gave me Zuri to love and have her as my own. What we did was consensual."

"How can a child give consent to something she knew nothing about? That shit is ludicrous and I don't care how you try to mix and match it to make that shit sound good. You were wrong for taking her innocence."

To my surprise, Zuri interrupted her rant. Tears were streaming down Mehzani's face as she yelled to get her point across. "It's true, sis. I was in love with Daddy and I initiated our first sexual encounter. It wasn't him." Zuri became emotional. "If you want to blame someone, blame me."

"Zuri, please." She held her hand up. "You did nothing wrong. As a father, it was his job to teach you right from wrong. Instead of having sex with you, he should've been telling you that was something shared between two adults. Not one adult and one child. That shit was sick and twisted."

"Mehzani, I prayed about it. I swear I did, but nothing would take away the desire I had for her."

"This is crazy. I can't listen to this anymore." Mehzani got up and stormed out of the camera's view.

Zuri had tears in her eyes, but they hadn't fallen yet. She had this evil look in her eyes and her next words sent my world tumbling down. "Mehzani is right. You were sick and twisted. You took advantage of the love I had for you."

Zuri's tears began to stream down her cheeks. "After today, don't ever call or reach out to me again, and I mean it. I never want to hear from you or see your face in this lifetime. You are dead to me. So leave me alone."

Daman nodded his head, wearing that same stupid, sarcastic smirk on his face. "Nah, it ain't Mehzani. It's that nigga and if you think you gone live happily ever after with him, you have another muthafuckin' thing coming. You might as well get ready for his funeral. Brick is dead and that's a promise."

"Fuck you, Daman. Go to hell and I hope you rot in that cell." Zuri hung up the phone, leaving me heartbroken and furious. I couldn't believe she just spoke to me in that manner. After all the shit we been through together, the promises and plans we made for the future, she would throw that away for some new nigga she barely knew.

I slung the phone hard across my cell and jumped up from the bed. Zuri had me fucked up and now somebody had to pay. On a mission, I left the room and went down to where they were playing cards. This dude owed me money and it was time to collect. I stepped to him with my chest puffed out.

"Where's the money you owe me?"

Steve looked up at me with a dumbfounded look on his face like I had two heads or some shit. "For real, man, you gone do this right here?"

"Right here, right now. You think I give a fuck about these niggas? Now, where my shit at?" I wouldn't care if the damn warden was present. His ass would've been getting an earful too.

"I don't have it." He looked away and went back to his game of spades, as if I wasn't standing there questioning him.

"So, when you gone have it?"

"I don't know." He shrugged his shoulders. "I'll pay you when I get it."

That fuck nigga had blatantly disrespected me and I couldn't have that shit. All it took was one fool to try you and from there it would be a domino effect. Nobody walking around that muthafuckin' compound was gone disrespect me and get away with it. Not that day, the next or in the future. Smoothly, I cocked my fist back and delivered a single blow to his mouth. Steve's body jerked as he fell backwards, landing on the floor.

"Fuck wrong wit' you? Don't you ever try me like that again." I stood over him and pounded my fist into his face repeatedly. The crowd of men surrounding us stood back and watched. Blood spewed from his mouth and nose, but I continued to demolish him until he stopped moving all together.

The commotion surrounding the fight caught the attention of the guards, because I could hear them calling my name. "Monroe. Monroe. Ya' ass going to the hole."

Someone grabbed me from behind and when I turned around to swing, it was one of the male officers. That didn't matter to me, because he could get it too. As soon as I popped his ass, two other officers jumped it in and tackled me to the ground.

"Take his black ass to the hole." one of them shouted.

"I don't give a fuck about a hole. Fuck y'all." Both officers dragged me out by my arms. I didn't give a fuck. When I got back out, I was gone be on savage mode, until Zuri came back to me. Until then, every nigga in my way was getting slaughtered.

***

Mehzani

It felt good to tell Daman how I really felt about his trifling, pedophile ways after all these years. That encounter was a long time coming. After I stormed off, I fixed me a drink and went out to catch a breather on the balcony. The view of the beach was relaxing and I was dying to get in the water.

As I thought back on our past, it made sense as to why Zuri was so defensive when it came to him. Daman had truly brainwashed my sister and she was too naïve to see otherwise. My heart genuinely ached for her and I regretted not figuring out the abuse earlier. Their bond always had me skeptical, because they were closer than we were and I was the baby. In fact, there were times I was jealous at the attention he gave Zuri. If I wasn't so busy thinking I was walking in her shadows, I could've helped her much sooner. That would be something I would regret for the rest of my life.

While I was admiring the view, I called to check up on Gucci to see if his condition improved. Sadly, he was still in the same shape I left him in. The thought of losing him made me sick on my stomach. I couldn't understand how someone like him could come into my life and leave so suddenly.

"How is your trip?" Melvin asked.

"It's good, but you know Gucci is on my mind, as usual."

Melvin sighed into the phone. "I know. Everything will be okay. Just be patient. I'm sure he'll be waking up soon."

The sliding door opened and when I turned around, Zuri was standing there with a distraught look on her face. Her eyes were pinkish, but she was no longer crying. "Are you okay?" she said softly.

"I'm fine, but I should be asking you the same thing. Give me one second though."

"I'll come back," Zuri insisted.

"No. I'm done. I was just checking on my boyfriend to make sure he was okay." I went back to Mel because I needed to talk to my sister. "Hey, I have to go, but call me if his condition changes."

"Okay. Have fun."

After I hung up the phone, I placed it on the small table. "Come and sit down. Let's talk."

Zuri walked over and sat down on one of the chairs. "This talk is long overdue."

"I agree." I sat down and took a sip from my drink. "Are you okay?"

Zuri nodded her head. "Honestly, I'm not. There's so much that has happened over the years and to this very day, you have no clue about the things I've been through."

When she said that, I felt it in my soul because the feeling was mutual. "Same here, but now we have each other to lean on. First, I want to say I'm sorry for snapping like that, but I've been carrying around that pain for years. There were so many times where I blamed myself for splitting up our family."

"No, Zhani. That wasn't your fault. We were doing things we shouldn't have been doing in the first place. It's my fault we crossed that line though."

"How? Daddy was a grown-ass man and he knew better. So, don't say that."

"It's true." She sniffled. "One night, I went into his room while he was asleep. He had been drinking, so he knocked out. I took it upon myself to climb into bed with him and give him head. When he woke up and saw me, he yelled at me and made me get out his room." Zuri started to cry, but she continued. "Do you know how that made me feel?"

Words couldn't describe how I was feeling at that moment. To hear her speak on such a disgusting act made my stomach turn. Of course, I wasn't going to say it because I wanted her to tell me what happened, so I took a gulp of my drink.

"No, I don't."

"I felt rejected and low. My own father denied me of the affection I thought I wanted."

"I'm confused, because you were young. How did you learn about that type of affection?"

Zuri sighed and looked away. Silence was amongst us for a good minute before she answered my question. "I used to see Legend and Shakira having sex and that made me curious."

"Damn," was all I could say, because that shit just blew me.

For the next hour, I sat and listened to Zuri go into complete detail about her relationship with our father. And to be honest, I had to say I was disgusted by it, but it all made sense to me. There was no justification for what went on, and at the end of the day Daman knew better, being that he was the adult in the situation. Not having a mother figure in our lives fucked my sister up big-time and for the first time, I was truly happy Daman and I were not that damn close. When Zuri finished her story, I went into full detail about mine, including my drug use and how Gucci saved me.

"Wait a minute." Zuri held her hand up in amusement. She was finally smiling. "You dating Gucci? Brick's cousin, Gucci?"

"Yes." I laughed. "It's so weird, because what if we would've met at a family BBQ or some shit?"

"That would've been funny as hell."

"I know, right?" The sound of his name rolling off my tongue was messing with me mentally, but I was trying to hold myself together, since we were past the crying stage. "I just hope he pulls through."

Zuri tilted her head to the side. "What do you mean?"

"He's in a medically induced coma. He was shot and he's not doing too well. They don't think he's going to make it, but he's still fighting. So, I am hoping for a miracle of some sort."

"Wow! I didn't know that. I'm so sorry you going through that. I really hope he pulls through."

"Me too. I don't know what I would do without him."

"Why did you agree to come to California?"

"Brick made me realize I couldn't stop the inevitable, and that both of us needed to get away and clear our heads from all of the tragedies we've been faced with."

"That's true." Zuri sighed. "We have been through a lot and from the look of things, I don't believe it's going to get any better."

"Why do you say that?" My curiosity was getting the best of me. I was more of an optimistic person in comparison to Zuri. It was like she was waiting on something to happen.

"I know Daman very well and I know this is not going to end well." Zuri had an emptiness in her eyes as she looked towards the beach with her head held low. "He's not going to let me go."

My heart sunk to my stomach, listening to her. Finally, she looked at me with buckets of tears in her eyes. "Not until he kills Brick."

Chapter 3

Coop

Danielle was out of the hospital and still aggravating as hell. I was trying to get some rest, but she was ruining that. One would think that she would appreciate me and life just a little bit more, after being involved in a near-death experience. But, oh boy, was I wrong. The little flesh wound didn't do shit except make her worse than before. Listening to all of her nagging made me wish it went just a little bit deeper, so she could stay in the hospital just a little bit longer. It was a terrible thing to say, but that's how I felt. Truthfully, she was starting to wear me down and marriage was slowly becoming something I no longer wanted.

"Would you stop ignoring me and answer my question?" Danielle pouted.

"What question?" My response was dry and I was hoping she realized I wasn't interested in having a conversation with her.

"Who the hell was shooting at you?"

"For the one hundredth time, I don't know and who said the hit was for me? It could've been Brick."

"Well, for one, Brick don't live here. For two, why would anyone look for him at our place? That doesn't make any sense to me."

"How about you ask the detective on the case? Because it damn sure ain't me." I rolled over on my side to keep from looking at her.

"I swear, you can be such a rude and insensitive jackass. I got shot because of some shit you did. As far as I know, it could've been somebody boyfriend or husband trying to take you out."

I exhaled loud and hard. "Do you ever just sit back and think about some of the shit you say? Everything reverts back to a woman, in your eyes."

"That's because you're a cheater and I despise that."

This conversation was about to take a turn for the worse and I felt that shit in my soul. Instead of keeping my back to her, I turned around so she could look me in the eyes once I defended myself.

"You say I'm a cheater and you don't trust me, but there's something that needs some clarification." I sat up in bed with my back against the headboard. "For me to be a cheater, it never stops you from sucking my dick every time I come in the house."

Danielle rolled her eyes, but she didn't respond.

"Don't get quiet now. I mean, what you trying to do, see if you can taste another bitch pussy juice on my shit?"

"Fuck no!" she snapped. "You always doing the most. I swear, that's why I can't stand you now."

"Danielle, the door is open and I swear I won't stop you this time."

The moment I was about to go in on her, my phone alerted me with a text message.

Brick: Meet me at the house in thirty minutes. The meeting is on with dude
Coop: Be there soon

I placed my phone on the nightstand and climbed from the bed. Finally, I was free from the wicked witch and I was happy to get away from her.

"That must be a bitch texting you."

Without a single word to her, I grabbed my phone and tossed it on the bed beside her, then walked off. Danielle was wrong all day. I wasn't cheating on her and I hadn't cheated since we got married, but all of that was about to change. She forced my hand, so I might as well do everything she accused me of, to make her accusations true. That night I chilled with the female I told Brick about, I really didn't smash, although I could've. The only reason I went there was because she wanted some weed and a molly, so I took it to her. We smoked and I passed out on the sofa. I took my vows serious and I really wanted to stay true to her, but I couldn't get no credit from her ass on any given day.

In the bathroom, I took a leak and washed my hands. When I came out, Danielle was doing exactly what I knew her to do. Scrolling through my phone, looking for nothing. I knew she read the text messages from the female, but there was nothing to see except her texts asking me to bring her some weed and pills. There was nothing that indicated we fucked or were interested in fucking for that matter. I really hoped she felt stupid.

"Are you done?" I walked up to her with my hand out.

Danielle handed me the phone. "You probably deleted everything you didn't want me to read."

That was a lie and I was tired of trying to prove myself to her over and over again. I grabbed my keys and headed towards the bedroom door, but before I walked through the door, I turned back to face her. "I really tried to be everything you wanted me to be, but that shit means nothing in your eyes. Contrary to your belief, I haven't fucked another female since we got married. I've been faithful to you all this time and I can see it was useless."

She rolled her eyes. "Yeah, okay."

"You don't have to believe it. As long as I know I did everything I promised you, I'm good with that and I'm done arguing with you about this. I hope you find what you looking for out in these streets, 'cause I'm good."

"What are you talking about?" Danielle's tone of voice changed quick from that snappy shit she was giving me seconds ago.

"I think it's best that we get a divorce. I'm tired of this and apparently, it ain't getting' no better, so it's best we go our separate ways. You can keep the place. I'll find me an apartment."

Danielle sat there in silence as I walked away and out of our condo. I knew she thought I was blowing smoke, but I really wasn't. There was only so much a person could do and I'd exercised all options. We didn't have any kids or property to divide, so we could easily go our separate ways. Danielle made her bed and now it was time for her to lay in it.

***

Brick

"What time this nigga coming?" We had been sitting up in that shop for over thirty minutes and I was tired of waiting.

"He said he'll be here in ten minutes," Mike replied, while looking down at his phone and swiveling back and forth in the chair behind the register.

"He need to hurry the fuck up. I got moves to make before it gets too late," Coop mumbled, loud enough for me to hear. Ever since we made it to the shop, his demeanor changed drastically.

"What's going on wit'cha, bruh? You been in a foul mood for a minute now. Talk to ya' boy." I leaned against the counter and folded my arms across my chest.

Coop looked at me, then over at Mike. "Aye, step out the room real quick. I need to holla at my nigga."

Mike walked into the back room and closed the door.

"What's the deal?" I was anxious to know what the lick read and who we needed to drop. My ace gazed into the window in deep thought, contemplating what he was about to say.

"I'm leaving Danielle," he blurted out.

"Wat'chu mean, you leaving sis?" That news threw me for a loop.

"I'm divorcing her. It's over, dawg. I can't do this shit no mo'."

He shook his head from side to side, while biting his bottom lip. I knew something serious had to happen if he was talking like that. And I also knew that shit wasn't smooth between them, but I figured they would get it together eventually. Apparently, I was wrong, and the situation was far worse than suspected.

"Yo' ass just talking right now."

"Dead-ass. That shit over with. I'm letting her keep the condo so she'll be straight, but I'm not going back."

"Nah, bruh. Don't throw in the towel just yet. I'm sure y'all can get through all of that. Just think about what you doin'." I tried to be his voice of reason, but I believed he had his mind made up long before we linked up.

"That shit dead. Ain't no going back after this." Coop took a deep breath, dragging his hand over his lips. "Dawg, when you do your best to make a muthafucka happy and they ain't never satisfied, that's a problem."

My eyes darted in his direction with a disapproving look, but he didn't give me a chance to speak.

"Bruh, don't even say it."

"What? I ain't say shit." I laughed.

"I already know what you gone say, so don't do it. Danielle knew what I was before we got married and she was good with that. I made her a promise I wouldn't cheat anymore, amongst some other shit and I've did just that. I haven't cheated, but no matter what I say or do, she don't believe me."

"I don't agree with that and you shouldn't give up so easily." He knew Danielle was crazy out the gate, but that wasn't an excuse for her behavior. And he also knew that he was to blame for that last episode by not going home.

Coop shrugged his shoulders. "I'm done trying to make her out of a believer. Issa wrap."

"Okay. I'm done." I held out my arms. "I don't have shit else to say about it, if that's what you wanna do."

"I 'preciate that."

The growling of an engine caused me to swivel my head to the left. "This better be that nigga, Raheem." I leaned up off the counter and looked at Coop. "Come on." Mike still had the door closed, so I opened it. "Aye, that nigga driving a Mustang?"

"Yeah."

"Well, get'cha fat ass out there and greet him." Coop pushed him in the back of the head. "Fuck you was doing back here, taking a lunch break, ole greedy-ass nigga?"

Mike didn't say anything. Instead, he proceeded to the counter to wait on Raheem to enter. When I heard the chimes on the door go off, I upped the strap just in case shit got rowdy. The door was slightly open, so we could hear the conversation.

"What's up, Big Mike? You ready to make that purchase?" Raheem stood with his arms folded. "I told you, you would be seeing me soon, so I hope you made a wise decision."

Mike placed both hands on the counter. "I told you, I have a distributor and I wasn't interested in changing. I've been dealing with them for a while and they do me decent."

Raheem took a step closer. "You think I give a fuck about a partnership y'all built? Fuck no. There's only two choices here and one of them has a fatal consequence." He pointed his trigger finger in Mike's direction. "And you don't want it to resort to that."

"Nah, you don't want to get in the way of my distro's money, 'cause he ain't having it. So again, I'm sorry, but I'm not interested in the position."

"Nigga, you think I give a fuck about Brick?" He shouted to the top of his lungs and hit his chest like King Kong. "Muthafuck Brick and everything he stand for. We run this shit. He think he can just come back and take over? It ain't happenin'."

At that point I heard enough, so I nudged Coop with my elbow and popped in on the meeting. My gun was aimed in his direction, as I took slow strides towards the counter. "And who the fuck gon' stop me?"

I stood beside Mike with a mean mug on my face and gritting my teeth. Coop was right at my side, ready to blast off and Raheem's boy had his piece out too. If a showdown was what they wanted, I was wit' it.

"I advise you to stop talking greasy and keep my name out yo' mouth. I'm running this shit now. So whatever you thought you was gon' do, you might as well dead it and take that shit back to Carolina, or whatever country-ass town you from. Ain't nobody moving in on my territory and live to tell the story."

Raheem laughed and looked back at his boy. "Yo, you hear this shit? This muthafucka been out for all of five minutes and think he can just come back and take over the south like that."

His boy nodded his head and chuckled. "He must be high on train smoke or some shit."

"Nah, but you gon' be high off gun smoke in a minute." That put an end to his laughter. "I don't have no problem starting a war in my own hometown, but you on the other hand, are a long way from home."

Raheem stood there for a minute, then rubbed his chin. "Okay, you win." He held up both arms. "I'll stay out the way."

"That's yo' best bet," Coop added, while still in position.

"We out." He looked over at his boy. "Let's hit it."

"No more warnings, so I suggest you stay out of my way." Raheem and his boy walked backwards towards the door, before exiting the same way they came in. We lowered our straps and tucked them away. Mike was still standing in place, like he was lost or in deep thought.

"Aye, Mike," I shouted.

"Yeah?" He snapped out of his daze.

"I suggest you invest in some security and stay strapped, nigga, just in case he feeling disobedient." Mike wasn't a killer, but sometimes those were the ones you had to watch out for. Especially if they felt like their lives were in danger, or they backed into a corner.

"Shit, if you feel that way, we should've murked the nigga right here," Coop suggested.

"It's a time and place for everything, son. Let's go. I'm on a mission right now."

"Y'all boys be easy," Mike hollered on our way out of his establishment.

"So, what mission you on?" Coop had a puzzled look on his face.

"I gotta go holla at Hector to check my car for a tracker. He thinks that's how I was located at your crib."

"Yeah, go handle that shit. I'm going to check on our money spots." Coop dapped me up.

"Bet. I'll hit you up to let you know what the business is." I went to my car, so I could get that shit handled ASAP.

Chapter 4

Skeet

"Yooo! The block swangin' hard, my nigga, like Jay Z and Beyoncé ticket sales during income tax time."

Kamari was happy as fuck to be my number-two. It wasn't official with Brick yet, but I knew he wouldn't say no. If I knew nothing else about my boss, I knew he was about his paper and anybody that was hungry. That was Kamari all day. And besides, Tone's ass was on his way out the door, so this was an easy replacement.

My nigga been solid since day one and I trusted him with my life. "Hell, yeah. They know black people gone spend that tax money quick. That nigga a genius fa' dat shit they pulled."

"I ain't mad at him. He know everybody splurge around that time of the year."

It was hotter than a sauna, but I had to get to the money. I sipped my Gatorade. "Well, all you gotta do now is give Brick that cash so he can put you on and then you can get to the money."

"I'm ready, shit. A nigga got summer goals."

"Fuck the summer. I got year-round goals. I'm ballin' twelve months out the year, three sixty-five and three sixty-six when it's leap year."

"Yeah, that sounds better than the summer."

The fiends were beating the block and we was passing that shit out like candy on Halloween night, for two hours straight. When the crowd died down, we stood on the sidewalk talking about nothing in particular, when a dark-colored van with tints pulled up. Two mixed dudes jumped out that bitch with DEA jackets on. My first thought was to run, but soon as I took a step, one of them muthafuckas pulled the strap.

"Don't do it or I'll blow your whole fuckin' back out and get away with it." He approached me slowly and I stood in place, completely frozen. What he was saying were actual facts and I had too much to live for. Therefore, I wasn't about to give him a reason to shoot. I didn't have any drugs on me and my gun was stashed in the bushes, so I wasn't worried about them sticking me with a real charge. When I looked over at Kamari, he was bent over with his hand over his mouth. I didn't know what the hell he was doing. Before I could say anything to him, they snatched both of us up at the same time and pushed us against the gate.

"Who y'all selling for?" the guy holding me asked.

"I don't know what the fuck you talkin' 'bout?" I snapped. This shit was crazy and if I found out who sent these crooked muthafuckas, they was getting they ass rocked.

"Don't play with us. Who the hell y'all selling dope for?" The one that was roughing up Kamari looked in my direction and mean-mugged me.

"I ain't selling shit," Kamari replied.

"Gone tell 'em, partner."

"Where is Brick?" I looked down at the ground and ignored his scratchy voice that was too close to my ear.

"I know you selling for him." He continued to poke at me for an answer.

"Who the fuck is that?" He was barking up the wrong tree if he thought I was about to tell him anything.

"How about you, middle school dropout?" They were looking at Kamari for an answer.

"Who is Brick?" Kamari asked in a low confusing tone.

"So, y'all both playing dumb. I advise y'all to save yourselves. When we take Brick down, we taking his whole crew. There will be no immunity when it's all over. It's now or never."

I put my arms behind my back and prepared for my arrest. "You might as well arrest me now, because I don't know what the hell y'all talking about.

Kamari seemed like he was nervous, but I had no way of verifying that. If he said anything, Brick was gone kill him and me and there was nothing I could do about it. They slapped the cuffs on and threw us in the back of the van.

"What the fuck y'all doing?" I blurted out in anger.

"Arresting y'all. What the fuck does it look like?" one of them shouted.

"Y'all muthafuckas ain't read me my rights or tell me what you getting me arrested for."

"Criminals don't have rights. Now sit back and shut the fuck up." One of them climbed in the back and hovered over Kamari while the other slammed the door shut before pulling off.

It was like the dude had it bad for Kamari. I didn't know if it was because he looked soft and they figured he would break easily, but, he wasn't letting up on my boy.

"So you wanna tell me now, before we get down to the station? Now is the time to free yourself. Don't listen to the idiot over there." He nodded in my direction. "He will be eating Ramen noodles for the rest of his life."

Kamari's head was down, but he looked up and glared at him eye to eye like a man. "Bruh, gone wit' all that 'cause I don't know who the fuck you talkin' 'bout."

Just as Kamari turned away, dude snatched him up by the collar and slung him against the metal floorboard. "Are you selling for Brick and I'm not gon' ask you no more?"

Kamari remained silent, so the DEA agent put his boot on the side of his face and pressed down on it. "Answer my fuckin' question."

"I don't know what the fuck you talking about." Kamari continued to keep his mouth shut.

The DEA agent hit the window. "Pull over."

A few seconds later, the van stopped and his partner opened up the door. "We got a tough one. Take his boy out and make him talk."

DEA officer number two pulled me out the van and slammed the door. "Where the fuck you taking me at, man?"

"Who is Brick?"

"Muthafucka, didn't I tell you I don't who the fuck he is? Y'all niggas don't listen for shit."

"You sure about that? 'Cause from what I'm hearing, you his number-two. So, you know what that means right? I get to bury your black ass under the prison."

"Don't count on that shit. You can't stick me with shit."

When I said that, he pulled his strap out on me and grinned at me menacingly. "Scream right now."

"What?" I looked at that nigga sideways like he was stupid. "Fuck you talkin' 'bout?"

"Open your mouth and scream before I put a bullet in your forehead."

That crazy-ass nigga fired the gun, so I screamed.

"Good. Now climb in the front and be quiet."

I didn't know what the hell they had going on, but soon enough I would find out. He opened the door and I climbed in, remaining silent until we pulled up to a tire shop and parked. DEA agent number two came around to my side and helped me out the van.

"Walk this way."

He pushed me in the back, but I didn't say shit. I just kept it moving. I was definitely taking notes because when I got loose and caught his ass on the rebound I was gone shove my gat down his throat and pull the trigger with no remorse. The place looked deserted, but I was ready to go into defense mode if need be. All I needed were those damn handcuffs off.

We walked up to a closed door. He knocked and opened it without waiting on a response.

"Get in there." He pushed me again. "You ready to meet your maker?"

I didn't know who the fuck he was bringing me to, but I kept my eyes on the chair, as it swiveled around slowly to expose the mystery person. When I saw his face, I had to admit I was relieved. This nigga was a damn fool.

"Bro, what the fuck, man?"

"That was a test, youngin'." Brick looked at me with a straight face. "And because you standing in front of me, it lets me know you passed." He looked at the agent. "Where's the other one?"

"They should be walking in now."

We could hear Kamari coming down the hallway. "Yo, where the fuck you taking me? And, what you did with my brother?"

"Shut the fuck up. You talk too damn much."

The agent pushed Kamari into the room with us. "Yo' Brick, you got you some solid workers. They passed."

"Uncuff them."

Kamari looked relieved. "Bruh, I'm happy to see you. I thought he murked yo' ass when I heard that gunshot."

"Shit, me too." It was okay to laugh now. A little while ago, I thought my ass was out of there.

They did as they were told and removed those tight-ass cuffs. My wrists were numb as fuck. I ignored the aches and sat down across from Brick. I had questions.

"Yo', these niggas real agents?"

"Nah. They a part of the Cuban Cartel."

That shit was crazy, but I was amused, yet impressed by my boss' connection. "Word?"

Kamari sat down beside me in the other chair while the fake DEA agents stood behind us.

"I see you passed my test." Brick nodded his head in approval at Kamari. "I ain't gon' lie, I thought you were gone fail when that pressure got on."

"I know the risks and I'm prepared to take my chances in order to get this money. You can trust me."

"Did you sell what I gave you?" Brick asked, referring to the coke he gave him.

"Almost. I have a few bags left," Kamari replied.

"Where are they?"

"I swallowed them."

"What?" Brick's eyes stretched wide in surprise. "Why the hell you swallowed it?"

"Them niggas jumped out too fast and I couldn't get caught with it."

"Go throw that shit up."

Kamari got up and walked to the trash can. We watched him as he stuck his finger down his throat. He gagged a few times before he threw up in the garbage.

Brick frowned. "Yo', take the bag out of there and go wash your hands. The bathroom down the hall on the right."

When Kamari walked out, I turned back to my boss. "So, what's next, you puttin' my boy on?"

"Yeah. He earned his spot."

Brick opened the drawer and pulled out a bottle of champagne and three goblets. He filled them and sat the custom glasses on the desk. My brother from another mother returned quickly with some napkins in his hand and took his seat.

"Grab your goblets." We did exactly what he said.

"Kamari, this here is a grown man's game and all I'm worried about is getting this money. We don't beef with one another and I don't tolerate any rats in my camp. I expect a lot and in return, you will be rewarded. If you don't think you can handle pushing large amounts of weight now is your time to bow out gracefully. If you ready say that shit."

"I'm ready."

"Raise your glasses." We held them in the air. "Kamari, welcome to Brick Money Boyz."

The boss turned his glass up first and we followed his lead. Brick downed that shit and sat his glass down. "Let's get to this money, young soldiers."

Chapter 5
Brick

Saturday night rolled around and I was done working, so I decided to drop in on Janae's party to see what was going on and to meet this Demarcus character. I wanted to bring Breanna with me, but I decided against it since I wasn't aware of what the crowd would be like. The majority were seniors in high school, and I wasn't too keen on having my innocent child around certain behavior. Everything she was going to learn was going to be on my watch.

From the road, I could see some of the fast-ass girls dancing and grinding on boys. Hence, why I didn't want to bring her. It made me laugh though, because it reminded me of when I was a teenage boy and attended house parties. The only difference was in my day, I wasn't doing no dancing. My ass was in the bedroom fucking and getting my dick sucked.

Stepping from my Benz, I clicked the locks and walked towards the house. The crowd of dirty dancers stopped to check me out. The new generation was fixated on material shit, so I knew they were checking out my threads, jewels and shoes. One of the boys looked me up and down, while nodding his head.

"Ayeee! What's up, Brick?" He had so much excitement in his voice.

I returned the nod, although I didn't recognize him. With me being a neighborhood legend, I wasn't surprised that he recognized me. "Coolin'."

I kept it moving to find Janae, but before I disappeared in the house, I could hear them talking.

"Yo' who is that nigga?" one of them asked.

"Dawg, you lame. That's Brick. That nigga like the Godfather of Lauderdale. I heard he was crazy as fuck, tho."

"What he doing here?"

"I think that's Nae daddy."

"Ohh."

When I walked into the house, I was impressed with the set-up and to see my money was used accordingly. Blue and silver balloons were everywhere. There was a candy table with all types of treats and a big ass cake with diamonds on it. She had a backdrop and all. Quickly, I spotted Janae in front of it, taking pictures with whom I presumed to be Demarcus. They were so damn close, it looked like he was painted on her backside. I stood there and observed them for a few minutes. After they were done getting their photos taken, they walked in my direction. Janae gave me the same look she did when I came to her job. I was standing there with my arms folded across my chest.

Janae stepped close to me and gave me a hug. "I'm so happy you made it. Be nice," she whispered.

"I had to."

She let me go and turned to face her boyfriend. "Bae this my daddy, Brick. Daddy, this is Demarcus." Janae smiled shyly as she referred to me as her father, instead of godfather. It wasn't uncommon, since I played a huge role in her life.

He extended his hand, so I grabbed ahold of it and squeezed it firmly. "Nice to meet you, sir. I've heard so much about you."

"Then you know I don't play when it comes to my daughter?"

Demarcus tried to hide his nervousness with his crooked smile as I held onto his hand. "Yes, I know. I've heard about you in the streets, not just from Janae."

From what I could see, he had done his homework. At the moment he seemed cool, but I would be checking him out on my own from the shadows. I let go of his hand and smiled at Janae.

"Where is your mother?"

"In the kitchen."

"Okay, don't get lost. I'll be back."

"Okay," she said sweetly.

Shannon was in the kitchen, standing at the sink, washing dishes and singing along with the music. "What's up, Shan?"

She turned around with a faint smile on her face. "Hey."

"You okay?"

"I don't feel too good, but I had to suck it up for my baby." She dried her hands with a dish towel while walking towards me. "I told Nae you wouldn't miss her special day."

Shan was a lot shorter than me, so I had to lean down and give her a hug. "I wouldn't have missed her party for the world."

"Thanks for everything. I don't know what we would without you."

"Don't sweat that. You know as long as I got it, y'all got it." That was my promise to her and I would always be there for them, no matter who was in my life. Whenever the time was right, I would tell Zuri about them. I didn't need any secrets between us on my behalf. I let Shan go and took a step back to check her out.

"How you doing?"

"I'm okay," she replied. "How are you?"

"I can't complain."

"And, how is Breanna?"

"She's good. I wanted to bring her, but I changed my mind." I leaned against the refrigerator.

"You gone have to bring her over here so I can see her. I'm glad you home, because Deja's crazy ass stopped letting me see her."

"She told me you stopped answering for her." I shook my head because that girl was silly as hell.

"Deja is a big ass liar. I called her one day and she told me I couldn't see her, because she heard me and you used to fuck around. I told her we were teenagers when that happened, and we hadn't slept together since back in the day." Shan put her hand on her hip. "But, of course, she didn't believe me. So, I was like fuck it. I'll just wait until you got home."

"I swear, that bitch need a head check. If my daughter wasn't here, I would regret the day I met that pussy-ass ho' and fucked her raw."

"No. I know she crazy, but don't talk about the mother of your child like that."

"Fuck her. That ho' ain't shit. You know she was fucking Gucci?"

Her eyebrows heightened in surprise. "Get the fuck out of here. Are you serious?"

"Hell yeah. They got a baby together too."

"How do you know?"

"Her mama told me she has a one-year-old and the rest came from the streets."

"Damn. She real nasty for that and Gucci ass ain't no better. I should've known something was up, because he was over there a little too much. But, I just blew it off like he was just there to help her."

Me and Shan always had a solid relationship, even after we stopped fucking. We grew up in the same neighborhood, so we hung out a lot. We were chilling at her house one early-release day and ended up losing our virginity to one another when I was fourteen. Shan was thirteen. Our first time was funny because I nutted so fast, but by the third round I was in there, killing the pussy. After that, we would meet up every day after school and have sex while her mama was at work. We had the same routine until my junior year in high school and I still hadn't technically made her my girlfriend. We just had that understanding.

Shit between us was smooth until she came to my high school her freshman year. That was when everything turned sour. Over the summer I had been smashing this chick and now we were all under the same roof. I was able to skate through for a few months before they caught wind of one another. Shan was hurt, because she saw it as me cheating on her, but I didn't see it that way back then. Shan stopped fucking with me altogether, but I still had my senior chick in place. She wasn't trying to go anywhere. A few months later, I found out Shan was kicking it with my boy, A.J. He stepped to me about it first, then Shan called me to come over so she could explain to me what happened between them. Of course, she made it out to be my fault, but I respected her honesty because she didn't owe me an explanation after the way I treated her. That was my loss, so I took that shit to the chin like a G and kept it moving, after she let me hit it one last time. That was the last time I ever slept with her.

"Did A.J. call Janae?"

Shan was wrapping up the food, as I watched. "Yeah, he called earlier to wish her a happy birthday. He sent her a card and his mama came over and brought her some money."

"That's good." Shan was moving slow, so I assumed she was in some type of pain. "You sure you okay?"

"My diabetes has been a little difficult to maintain lately." Her eyes shifted towards the floor, as she held on to the counter.

I hated to see her like that, so I embraced her in my arms. "I'm sorry to hear that. Damn." I sighed, holding her tight in my arms. "If you need anything, let me know. I don't care what it is or what time of day or night it is. Call me."

"Okay." She nodded her head and I heard a sniffle. "Thank you."

"You don't have to thank me."

"Yes, I do. You do more than what's asked of you."

"I owe you that much," I honestly stated.

"You don't owe me anything."

"Yeah, whatever." I let her go and looked into her round, sullen eyes. "Are you getting the proper treatment? Do you have insurance?"

Shan giggled. "Slow down, Brick. My insurance pays for everything."

"Okay, but I meant what I said."

"I know and that's why I love you."

"I love you too." That was the truth. I loved her, but I wasn't in love with her. What we had was a thing of the past, but I would always feel bad for the way I treated her when we were younger.

"Look at you, getting soft." Shan tried smiling through the pain.

"I always told you I love you."

"I know."

My phone vibrated in my pocket, shifting my focus away from Shan. When I pulled it out, it was just who I was waiting on.

"Sup."

"I'm outside," Coop replied.

"Okay. I'm coming out now." I ended the call, put it back in my pocket and grabbed Shan's hand. "Let's go find Janae."

Janae was in the backyard laughing and talking amongst her friends when we walked up. Demarcus wasn't too far away. "Come with us," I instructed her.

"What's wrong?" She panicked and held her chest as if something was wrong. "Ma, you okay?"

"Yeah, she's fine. I have someone I want you to meet."

"Okay." That calmed her down.

Janae followed behind us as we headed to the front yard. Coop was waiting for us by the road, with a silly smirk on his face. She looked at us with her nose tooted up. "I know this not who you want me to see?" She snapped her neck in my direction. "I thought you wanted me to meet your girlfriend or something."

Coop shook his head and laughed. "You should be happy to see me, ol' peanut-head-ass girl."

Janae could no longer hold in her laugh. "I swear I can't stand you."

"Yeah, I love you too." Coop handed her two, one-hundred-dollar bills. "Happy birthday."

"Thank you, big head." Janae smiled and gave him a hug.

"You welcome." Coop looked in my direction. "How you doing, Shan?"

"I'm good and you?"

"Shit, I'm hanging in there."

"That's good," Shan replied.

Coop slid me the keys and I handed them off to Janae. "Happy birthday."

Janae's face lit up with excitement. "No, you didn't." She screeched, "I know you didn't buy me a car?"

"Click the button." It made me happy to see her smile like that. Today was a special moment that her father should've been home for, but as her godfather, it was my job to make sure she smiled in his absence.

Janae hit the keypad and rushed towards her brand-new 2018 blue Maxima. With her safety in mind, I opted out of getting her a luxury vehicle. The car I purchased was luxurious enough for a college student, especially when she wasn't paying for it. I walked up behind her as she checked out the inside.

"Do you like it?"

"Omgeeee, I love it." The tone of her voice confirmed the words she spoke. Janae got out the car and hugged me once more. "Thank you so much. You are the best substitute dad a girl could ever dream of. This means so much to me."

"You're welcome."

Holding her in my arms made me think about the things I had to look forward to in the future with Breanna. I missed my baby and I was definitely going to get her the next day.

"Nothing you do seems to amaze me." Shan placed her arm on my shoulder. "From the bottom of my heart, I appreciate everything you've ever done for her without me having to ask."

Janae broke our hug and when she looked me in the face, she had tears in her eyes. "I'm so happy right now."

"Stop crying and go enjoy your party." I knew she would love it, but I didn't expect her to cry.

Coop and I stayed until the party was over to help Shan with the clean-up. With the help of Nae's friends, we were able to clean up house in one hour, tops. My ass was tired, breathing all hard and shit, when I flopped down on the sofa to rest my feet.

Coop joined me. "I ain't sign up for this shit, Shan!" he shouted. "You owe me big time. I'm too old for this shit."

Shan laughed. "The one you sitting beside is gone pay you." Just like me, Coop grew up with Shan as well, and we all stayed close over the years.

"I ain't gone hold my breath on that shit," he huffed.

"You better not, 'cause you'll be a stiff ass waiting on me to pay you for cleaning up."

Coop stood up. "I'm out. This damn coo-coo outside blowing the horn."

"You got some bionic ass ears, 'cause I ain't hear shit." I stood up to leave as well.

"Brick, can you stay for a few? I need to talk to you about something," Shan blurted out.

Coop stopped in his tracks and turned back to look at us. "Yeah, I bet you do," he snickered.

"Get your mind out the gutter, because it's not like that. I need to talk to him about a personal matter."

"Hey," I interrupted. "You ain't got to explain shit to that nigga. Get'cha ass out of here before Danielle get out and embarrass you. Then you gone be in the dog house again."

"Don't worry about me, 'cause yo' ass next after you leave here tonight." Coop walked out and closed the door behind him.

All night it seemed like she had so much on her mind, but I had no clue as to what she could possibly want to tell me. However, I was about to find out shortly.

"Thank you for not mentioning my weight loss. This hasn't been easy for me. I've been struggling with saying something, but I know I need to tell somebody."

"What's going on with you?"

Shan grabbed my hand and at the drop of a dime, she just broke down and started crying. I knew whatever she had to tell me was bad news and I needed to brace myself for the worst. I was happy Janae wasn't there to witness any of it.

Chapter 6

Deja

My life was certainly not going as planned and I hated that shit with a passion. Somebody was definitely praying on my downfall and they was winning. Right about now, Gucci was supposed to be in utter bliss, raising our son together and living happily ever. But no, he wanted to be laid up with a fucking junkie-ass bitch that was hooked on flakka. He stayed trying to be Captain Save a Ho' with his ol' Captain Kirk ass.

I knew for a fact he was Jace's father, which was why he had my last name. When it all boiled down to Breanna, I was almost certain Brick was her father, but there was a slight possibility she wasn't. Genetically speaking, it was hard to tell because of the strong resemblance between the cousins.

The original plan was to sit down with Brick and come clean about what happened while he was locked up. I wasn't going to mention the fact that we fucked on numerous occasions before he went in, because that was irrelevant. My mind kept telling me to not bring up old rubbish and leave that in the past. There was never any questions about paternity and sure as hell wasn't about to bring that up. Brick was pink slip, Henderson Clinic crazy, and I didn't need those problems in my life.

It took me a while to build up the nerve to tell him the truth, out of fear of how he would retaliate. We both figured it would be easier to tell him it wasn't intentional between us, and that our closeness was what pulled us into bed with one another. Now that was a thing of the past, because Gucci completely flaked on me right after Brick said he wanted nothing else to do with me, and he hated my guts for keeping Breanna away from him. I found it very funny that he suddenly had a heart and felt bad for sleeping with me. I called bullshit, but I had no proof if that's how he really felt, besides the fact that he cut me off.

When I found out I was pregnant, he told me to get an abortion and that was all the proof I needed. But, the way I felt about Gucci wouldn't allow me to kill his child. I loved him, but I also wanted to hurt Brick in the process for sleeping with that bitch, Dana. She and I weren't the best of friends, but we had a work relationship and it was foul on their behalf to even cross that line.

I stood in the mirror with an evil look on my face. It made me angry that Gucci lied to me. He tricked me into believing we would be together. That nigga had me feeling stupid, especially when he tried to front on me in front of his junkie bitch. Those two cousins were one and the same, but some of their characteristics made them different. Brick was mean as a rattlesnake, but he always took care of home. When he loved, he loved hard and he showed how much he loved you. Gucci, on the other hand, was more of a pushover when he finally let a woman inside his world. That wasn't an easy task though, because he was big-ass male whore.

Things weren't always bad between Brick and I and I dreamed about being with him forever. He just had to ruin it when he cheated on me. I was never able to forgive him for that and on top of that, he had the nerve to have Breanna around Shannon. He was dead-ass wrong for taking my daughter to a bitch house that he used to fuck. Goddaughter my ass, he was still fucking that girl and he could save that lie for a bitch that believed it, because I sure as hell didn't. My mind was set on getting revenge for breaking my heart. Brick was the reason I was a woman scorned and Gucci only added fuel to the fire.

The knock on the door put an end to my trip down memory lane. Quickly, I tossed my towel onto the dresser and slipped into a dress. I splashed on some body mist before going into the living room, where Breanna was watching cartoons. I unlocked the door and opened it. Kenny was standing there with a big ass grin on his face, with Jace in his arms.

"What's up baby mama?" he asked.

"Horny as fuck." I took Jace from his arms and kissed him on the cheek. "Hey, fat man."

Jace smiled just like his real daddy and that broke my heart, because he was being raised by a man who *thought* he was the father. It wasn't right, but if Gucci didn't want us as a package deal then he couldn't have either one of us. It was probably petty, but I didn't give a fuck. If he ever came to his senses and we got back together, then he could be in his son's life. Until then, my son will never meet him. I walked over to where Breanna was sitting and sat the baby beside her.

"Bre, watch your brother." That little girl had the nerve to roll her eyes at me.

"I'm not his mama." She ignored the fact that I was standing there and continued watching cartoons. "My daddy said I can't have kids."

Before I knew it, I slapped her ass in the mouth and she started crying. "Girl, please. I don't give a damn about what your daddy said, fuck him."

"Why you hit that damn baby like that, man? You trippin' for real and stop saying, 'fuck her daddy.' That shit ain't cool."

"Shut up, girl." I turned to face him. "Mind your business and worry about your own child."

"Shidd, they look twins to me. You sure I'm his daddy?"

"You know damn well her daddy was in prison when I got pregnant, so stop playing with me."

"Chill out, damn. I was joking."

"Sure you was."

My eyes were like slits when I mugged his stupid ass. He always had some slick to say. Kenny better hope Gucci never changed his mind, because I would burst his bubble quick about him not being the daddy. Kenny placed both hands on my hips and pulled me close to him, so I could feel his dick against my thigh.

"Let's make another one." He kissed my neck, then rolled his tongue around my earlobe. I was hot and bothered so I led him to a familiar place, my bedroom, to put out the blazing fire between my legs.

"Close the door and make sure you lock it," I demanded, while slipping off my dress. The last thing I needed was an interruption by a slick mouthed six-year-old. As childish as it may seem, I was pissed off at what she said. That made me wonder what he been saying around her. Bre acted like Brick was Jesus Christ or some shit.

Anxiously, I crawled into the bed and waited on Kenny to get naked, with his cute, red ass. He was a smaller version of Kevin Gates with dreads. I opened my legs and patted my pussy. That bitch was hot and ready, like Little Caesar's. It had been a minute since I had my shit beat up and I was ready for some penetration, straight pound action.

Kenny wanted us to be together for the longest time, but after I kept saying no, he finally stopped bringing it up. He probably had another bitch by now, but I didn't care. All I wanted was some hard dick and money from him. That was it. Unbeknownst to him, I only slept with him on the rebound, because of the shit I was going through with Gucci.

He crawled on top of me and I could feel his rock-hard dick press against my lips and make its way down my slippery slope. That first thrust was a breath of fresh air.

"Yesss," I exhaled heavily.

Kenny pushed my legs back, but kept his hands on my knees, as he thrusted in and out my pussy. Pinning me down and pounding my cat just so happened to be his favorite position. That gave him a sense of control, since he couldn't handle me any other time with my reckless mouth. Every time we had an argument and sex followed, he would take it out on me sexually. And each time he did, I was at his mercy.

"Yeah. Yeah."

My knees were damn near touching the bed. He had my ass spread full-length to keep me from moving. I couldn't close my legs if I wanted to. Kenny drilled me hard with long strokes, fucking my stomach up.

"Ah. Ah. Ah." My lungs were going crazy in my chest with every scream. It was like they were rattling.

"Yeah. What's that shit you was talking a lil while ago?"

My screams wouldn't allow me to respond. I'll save my slick rap for later. In the meantime, I took that dick the way I always did.

"Ooh. Ooh. Ooh." I placed my hand on my pussy and rubbed it while he punished her with every deep, hard stroke. The bottom of my stomach was in pain like a muthafucka, but I didn't want him to stop.

"Talk that shit now wit' yo' tough ass." Our skin collided with every thrust, causing a smacking noise. "A nigga put that dick on ya' ass and you can't talk."

My hand was working overtime to get a good orgasm. There was nothing that felt better than cumming long and hard when the pressure was being applied. Kenny hit that spot and I couldn't help but sing myself into a full orgasm. That shit felt so good, we fucked for another hour.

I was on top riding him hard like a horse, while he played with the clit. That shit was so hot and steamy. I didn't want it to come to an end. Leaning forward, I bounced hard on it. Kenny matched my thrusts. Suddenly, the loud banging on my room door scared the shit out of me. I knew it wasn't Bre, because it was too hard.

"Who the fuck is that?" Kenny asked.

"I don't know." My first thought was that Breanna had let Brick in. "Who is it?"

"The neighbor. You need to get out here now," someone screamed.

I jumped up and tossed my dress back on and rushed to open the door. The man who lived next to me was standing in my hallway, with a distraught look on his face.

"What's going on?" I questioned him, but furthermore, I wanted to know how in the hell he got in my house.

"Come quick, something happened." He turned on his heels and rushed towards the front door.

When I stepped onto the front porch, a crowd of people were outside hollering and screaming. Sirens could be heard nearby. I followed him towards the commotion and I heard a lady screaming, "I'm so sorry. I'm so sorry. I didn't see her."

As I walked up, everyone was staring at me. One lady stepped to the side and my heart dropped, splattering all over the concrete. Breanna was lying on the road, unconscious, with blood on her face and head.

"Noo!" I screamed, falling down to my knees beside her and cradling my precious baby in my arms. "Breanna, wake up, baby please." Tears streamed down my face as I rocked her in my arms, until the paramedics pried my baby out my arms.

Kenny was standing beside me, rubbing my shoulders while I watched helplessly as they tried to resuscitate Bre.

"She has a pulse. Let's hurry up and get her to the hospital," one of the medics shouted.

"Ride with her and I will follow them."

In a hurry, they put her inside the ambulance. I joined them, because there was no way I would let my baby be alone. On the way to the hospital, I prayed hard that she would pull through. If Breanna didn't make it, I would never forgive myself. The guilt was weighing down on me heavy, because while I was too busy trying to get some dick, my fuckin' daughter got hit by a car. I already knew Brick was going to call me every bitch, ho' and any other degrading name he could call me. And, in all honesty, I wouldn't blame him. *What type of mother was I to allow this to happen on my watch?*

***

When we made it to the hospital, they made me sit in the waiting room, as they operated on my baby. Kenny was there to comfort me. He also brought my cellphone because I'd left everything. I'd even left the front door open. At any second, Brick was due to arrive because I sent him a text. What I didn't do was tell him she got hit by a car. I simply stated she was in the hospital and to get here pronto. God was gone have to send me a boat load of angels to protect me from Brick. He loved Breanna more than he loved any person or thing on the planet. To be honest, I was scared to death about what he would do to me at this point.

"What the fuck happened to my daughter? And where is she?" Brick came through at a high rate of speed, shouting loud as hell, and I could feel all the life leave my body.

Chapter 7

Brick

This dumb ass ho' had the nerve to be in the hospital with the next nigga. He was holding the baby in his arms. I wanted to slap the shit out of her.

"You hear me talking to you?" I shouted once more. "What the fuck happened to my daughter?"

Deja was sitting there crying. Dude stood up and tried to shake my hand, but I looked at his shit like it was dirty. "I'm Kenny. Her baby daddy."

"I ain't in the mood for no introductions. My only concern is my daughter, so if you ain't trying to tell me what happened, then step," I growled.

Kenny dropped his hand. "I know you upset, but she is too. Take it easy on her."

"I don't give a fuck about that. What the fuck happened to my child? I'm not asking no more."

"She got hit by a car." He let that shit roll off his tongue quick.

My pressure shot straight through the roof and I could my body grow weak. I stepped to Deja, getting up in her face. "How did my baby get hit by a fuckin' car? Where the fuck was you?"

Deja sobbed and rocked in the chair. "It all happened so fast. I don't know."

"You better give me better answers than that, before I fuck you up in this hospital and put you in ICU." I snatched her up by her collar. "Bitch, what the fuck happened?"

Kenny grabbed my hand to keep me from choking the bitch out, but I pulled away from him. "Get yo' fuckin' hands off of me."

"A'ight, bruh. I'm just trying to get you to calm down. It's a stressful situation and this ain't helping neither one of y'all."

I heard what he was saying, but it ain't mean shit. I had zero understanding when it came to mine and that was a fact. The sound of footsteps behind me caused me to turn around. It was a doctor.

"Hello, I'm Doctor Frazier. Are you the parents of Breanna Riccardo?"

"Yeah, I am." I spoke up. My heart panged with heartache as I waited to see what he was about to say. The last time I felt like that was when my mother passed away. "What's going on with my baby?"

"Well," he sighed. "She has a broken leg and a head injury. I stitched up the gash on her forehead and she's resting right now. There was also some internal bleeding that I was able to control, but she's going to need a blood transfusion."

"Is she going to be okay?" I couldn't believe my child was lying up in a hospital bed.

"Hopefully, she will be. Are you able to donate blood?"

"Whatever she needs, I got it." I didn't give a fuck if my baby needed a kidney or lung, she could have it.

"Okay, I need to prep you for it, so come this way."

I followed the doctor to a cold and sterile room. "Have a seat." He sat down and pulled out a form. "The first step is blood-typing. You and the patient have to be a match in order for this to work." He paused for a second. "You are the child's biological father, right?"

"After six years, I better be." If this procedure didn't work because we're not a match, God was my witness. Deja was gone die that very day. I'd spend the rest of my life in prison if I had to.

"Okay. I'm just asking before we get started. If the blood isn't a match, that would be risky for the patient and she could suffer from hemolytic reaction."

I nodded my head to let him know I understood.

"Cross-matching would be the second step. What that means is that we would take both blood samples, and screen them for specific antibodies to avoid a reaction. I need you to read and sign the consent form to indicate you understand the procedure, risks and benefits of doing this."

"Okay." The doctor handed me the paper and I immediately read through it, before signing my name on the dotted line and handing it back to him.

"Now, the next step is to take your vital signs. I'm going to have a nurse come in and do that. She will then hook you up to a machine that will draw your blood."

"Okay."

"I'll be right back."

The doctor left the room and my thoughts were all over the place. I dropped my head in my hands and prayed harder than I did the night I left Breanna to kill Legend. That girl was my whole entire world. I couldn't live without her and I meant that shit. If my baby died, her mammy was going too. That was a promise. Zuri would be okay without me. A few minutes later, the doctor returned with a nurse.

"Mr. Riccardo, this is Nurse Sonya and she's going to start the process with you. If you have any questions, ask her."

"Okay."

"I'm going to check on your daughter," he said, before leaving me alone with the chocolate-covered nurse. Her melanin was definitely poppin' and she reminded me of my mother, with her flawless skin and perfect white teeth.

"Okay, Mr. Riccardo, let's get started." I watched as she washed her hands and place a pair of vinyl gloves on for protection. "I'm going to place an intravenous catheter in your arm to draw the blood, after I check your vital signs."

I nodded my head in approval.

Nurse Sonya walked me through each step as she checked my blood pressure and heart rate. When she was done, she pulled out a bag, needle and some other shit that made my skin crawl. It looked as if she was prepping me to shoot up or some shit. I hated needles, but for my daughter's sake, I would do whatever it took to keep her alive. The nurse tied the large rubber band around my arm and picked up the needle.

"You will feel a little pinch."

"Hold up. Do you know what you doing?" I knew she was a nurse, but I needed to know he didn't hook me up with a rookie.

Nurse Sonya shot daggers in my direction, then laughed it off. "Boy, I've been drawing blood before you even thought of coming out your daddy's nut sack. I'm a professional." She placed her hand on her hip. "And I know you not scared of needles, with all those damn tattoos on your arms."

Man, that shit she said took me out and I couldn't help but to laugh at her sense of humor. "Okay, I apologize. Do ya' thang."

"Thank you."

As promised, it was painless and I was officially hooked up successfully and making progress to save my princess' life. Once the blood bag was filled, she disconnected me from the machine and placed a bandage on my arm.

"Now, that wasn't so bad, was it?" Nurse Sonya smiled.

"No it wasn't. Thank you."

"You're welcome." She grabbed the bag. "Hang tight while we screen the blood and check for antibodies. Once we make sure the blood matches, we'll start the transfusion."

"How long does that take?"

"It could take up to two hours, as long as she doesn't have a reaction to it. I'll keep you abreast of what's going on, but in the meantime, go down and get you something to drink."

"Please save my baby," I pleaded.

"I'll do everything I can to save that beautiful baby girl of yours. Just stay strong for her sake."

"I'll do my best."

When I went back out to the waiting room, Deja was still sitting there looking stupid. Kenny was no longer sitting there. "How did it go?" The nervousness was so loud in her voice that I could hear her voice box shake.

"If my baby dies, just know that you joining her and I put that on my dead mama's grave." With that being said, I walked off to go downstairs and get me something to drink from McDonald's.

Two hours had passed and I was anxious as hell. The nurse said it could take up to two hours, but she hadn't come to the waiting room yet. My heart was telling me everything was okay, but my mind was telling me that anything could be happening. As far as I knew my baby could be laying on a cold slab. The waiting game was driving me insane, but I sat there and waited not so patiently with my headphones in my ear and my eyes closed.

Plain as day, I watched Nurse Sonya walk up to me with sadness in her eyes and her hands shoved down in her jacket. It looked as if she had been crying. I immediately jumped to my feet. "Is she okay?"

"Mr. Riccardo, I'm sorry, but Breanna didn't make it."

"What?" At that moment, my whole world crashed and all I could think of was killing Deja, right there in that hospital.

"After we did the transfusion, she had a reverse reaction and her lungs collapsed. I'm so sorry for your loss."

"Yeah, me too." I walked in slow motion towards Deja. The moment I was in front of her, I reached out and grabbed her by the neck. My grip was tight and squeezed as hard as I could. The nurse was standing behind me screaming for help, but I didn't care. *Who the fuck was going to help me since I lost my daughter?* Nobody. I was ready to go to prison for the remainder of my days. The life I once knew no longer existed the second my daughter took her last breath.

Deja gasped for air and clawed at my hands, but I wasn't letting up. "Die bitch, die," I spat over and over again. Someone tried grabbing me, but I was like the Incredible Hulk. I couldn't be moved at all. My goal was to kill the bitch in the same hospital my daughter was born in and died in.

It took a minute for her movement to slow down. I watched closely as her eyes rolled to the back of her head and her breathing became shallow. That made me squeeze her throat so hard, I heard and felt her neck snap beneath my fingers. That moment made me happy and I let her body drop hard to the floor.

"I told you I was gone kill you if my daughter didn't make it, bitch." I spit in her face before I stood erect, while I continued to stare down at her, happy with my revenge.

"Don't move!"

"Freeze!"

The commands were simultaneous and when I looked to where the sounds were coming from, I saw three police officers with their weapons aimed in my direction. I raised both hands in the air so they could see I was no longer a threat.

"Arrest me. I killed her."

Tears streamed down my face and my breathing was heavy. All I could hear was Breanna's happy laughs in my ear. I just wanted to hear that again and there was only one way that would happen. My well-being no longer mattered since my heart had been ripped out of my chest. There was only one thing that would make me happy and that was being with my princess. Lowering my hands, I reached behind my back for a weapon that wasn't there. I knew what was about to happen and it was what I wanted.

Multiple gunshots rang out in the waiting room and I felt several bullets rip through my chest. The sensation was hot, but I was numb to the pain. In slow motion, my body collapsed to the floor. Blood spilled from my mouth onto the tiled floor as my teary eyes fluttered, while my spirit slowly left my body. My heartbeat was loud, yet weak and I saw a bright light ahead of me. There was a little girl standing in an all-white gown reaching out to me.

"Daddy, please don't go, I need you." It was Bre. "Daddy, please wake up. Please," she begged. "Don't leave me alone." My heart stopped beating and the last gust of wind left my mouth like weed smoke. Then, I saw my mother welcoming me with open arms and I smiled.

"Mr. Riccardo. Mr. Riccardo. Are you okay?" I could feel someone shaking my body hard. "Wake up."

When I opened up my eyes, I felt disoriented, like I had been drinking. Sweat was protruding from my forehead as I wiped it away. I looked around and Deja was sitting there, very much alive. Nurse Sonya was standing in front of me, so I removed my headphones from my ears to see what she had to say. Deja walked over so she could hear as well.

"You were dreaming. Are you okay?"

"Um. I," I stammered over my words and took a deep breath. "I. I'm okay. How is she?"

"When we started the transfusion, she had a mild allergic reaction that resulted in hives and a slight fever. We gave her diphenhydramine to treat the symptoms and continued the transfusion."

"What does that mean?" I needed her to get to the point. "Did the transfusion work? Is she going to be okay?"

"Yes. Everything is going well. She's not awake yet, but eventually she will wake up."

A sigh of relief took over my body and I could jump for joy, knowing my baby was going to pull through. "I need to see her."

"Sure thing."

"I need to see her too," Deja spoke up.

"Are you her mother?" Nurse Sonya asked, with a look of uncertainty on her face.

"Yes."

"Okay, right this way and please leave the baby." Deja handed the baby to that duck ass nigga.

As bad as I wanted to stop her from coming in with me, I remained silent. It was her fault we were in there to begin with. If she was responsible, the way a mother should be, Breanna wouldn't be fighting for her life.

Nurse Sonya walked us into the pediatric wing of the hospital and into the private room where she was being kept. Breanna looked extremely peaceful as she slept. It pained me to see her in that condition. Her tiny arm housed the same needle and tubes as mine did earlier. My baby's leg was in a cast, her ponytails were disheveled and her face was slightly bruised. The doctor warned me that she had stitches on her forehead, but that didn't make me feel better.

I stroked the top of her head gently. "I'm so sorry, baby. Something kept telling me to pick you up last night. I wish I would've followed my first mind. This would've never happened to you."

Tears rolled down my cheeks as I watched her take tiny breaths. After today, I was going to take being overprotective to the extreme. I refused to let her out of my sight, except when she went to school or when I had to work. I was going to make sure nothing else happened to my child. It was my job to protect her and I felt as if I failed to do that. Granted, I wasn't there, but I still felt responsible.

Deja placed her hand on Bre's arm and it pissed me off. "What the fuck you crying for? This is your fault."

"Brick, don't start. I already feel bad enough, so I don't need your help in making me feel worst."

"I don't give a fuck about your feelings. You probably was sucking dick, while my daughter was outside playing alone and walked out in that road."

Deja shook her head. "You don't care what come out your mouth."

"And you don't care what goes in yours."

"Whatever."

"You didn't deny it, so it must be true."

She wouldn't look me in the face for shit. "This is not the time or place for this, so just stop before this escalates for no reason."

"I know one thing, yo' ass better be lucky our blood type was a match, 'cause you would be laying on a cold slab right now. So, if Gucci ever comes out his coma, you can let him know that he not the daddy since there was confusion."

Deja remained silent and I continued to talk to my baby. "Daddy is here now, princess, and after today I promise nothing like this will ever happen on my watch. I promise you that. I'm going to fight for you to make sure I have access to you at all times."

"And exactly what do you mean by that?" Deja rolled her neck.

"Exactly what I said."

"You have access to her now, so I'm confused."

"What's new?" I slickly stated.

"I swear, you get on my nerves." She rolled her eyes.

"I'm filing for custody of my daughter is what I mean. Do you understand that?"

"No you not. She gone stay right where she's at."

"You got me fucked up if you think I'm letting her come back to your house. You don't want her, so stop the bullshit. The only thing you worried about is keep that Section-8. If it wasn't for that, you wouldn't give a fuck if I took her or not."

"I love my daughter whether you believe that or not, and you can stop saying I only want her for benefits, because that's not true."

"Yeah, yeah. You better put Junior on your lease so you can keep it. The day she get out this hospital, I will be taking her home with me and you can bet that."

"I didn't say you couldn't take her. I'm just saying I'm not allowing you take custody from me. That's crazy for you to even say that. I took care of her while you were in prison for five years. No one helped me. I did that."

"Get the fuck out of here. Gucci, Coop, and Shan helped you with her, so you can stop with the lies. Gucci just gave you more than the others and you stopped Shan, 'cause you thought we was still fucking. Just so you know, I ain't fuck Shan since we was in high school."

"Yeah, I bet."

"Oh, if I did, I would gladly say it right now and you know it."

"Brick, I don't care. You can fuck whoever you want to."

"Good, just worry about this paperwork I'm about file."

"You are so nasty."

"When it comes to her," I nodded my head towards Breanna, "I'll turn into Lucifer."

Nurse Sonya peeked into the room before walking in. "Is everything okay in here? I could hear you two arguing from the hallway."

"No. He's a problem," Deja snapped.

"I'm afraid I'm going to have to ask you to leave, so Breanna can get her rest. Her rest is crucial to her healing process. The both of you are more than welcome to come back in the morning."

Today was that bitch's lucky day, but she was gone see me soon enough for this shit she just pulled. On my way out the hospital, Coop hit my line.

"Yeah," I answered with a flat tone.

"Aye, bruh, you need to go handle that nigga Tone ASAP, before I do it," he shouted into the phone.

"What the fuck going on?

"This nigga higher than Cooter Brown on our shit. I told you not to give that junkie-ass muthafucka another chance."

"I'ma handle the shit right now. Chill the fuck out."

"I'll be waiting."

"Where you at?"

"Parked by the nigga house." Coop was so pissed I could hear the hostility in his voice.

"I'm on my way."

I hung up the phone and jogged to my car. Before I got inside, I popped the trunk to grab the goods. Twenty minutes later, I was pulling up behind Coop's car. I walked up to his car with a small black bag in my hand and got inside.

"What the fuck going on?" I asked once more.

"I told you, now let's go in here and smoke this muthafucka. We losing money behind him. That nigga ain't 'bout his business. He supposed to be flooding the streets, not his muthafuckin' nose."

"Bruh, chill the fuck out. I got enough shit going on and I don't need the additional stress. I'm 'bout to handle this shit right now." Coop looked at me with worry in his eyes. "What's going on, bruh?"

His question triggered my emotions and I choked up instantly. Shaking my head, I turned my head revealing the tiny slits on my face. My mind and body was drained. "Breanna got hit by a car today and she's in stable condition, bruh."

Tears slid down my face, thinking about my innocent child lying in that hospital bed, fighting to live. "This ho' wasn't watching my baby, man."

"Damn, bruh, I'm sorry to hear that. What you gone do 'bout that? That's some reckless ass shit."

"Yeah. I know this ho' was getting fucked while my daughter was outside by herself."

"You sure 'bout that?"

"She was at the hospital with the nigga when I got there. Why else would he be up there, unless he was with her? After we leave here, I need to go by there. I know somebody saw something."

"Whatever you wanna do, I'm wit' you."

"Let's go." We slid out the car in silence and stepped up on the porch. The lights were on and I could hear moaning. The dumb muthafucka left the door open, giving us easy access.

Some crackhead ho' had her head between his legs, giving him dome. He was so loaded he didn't know we were standing there. We watched closely as he sprinkled powder on his dick. She licked that muthafucka clean off. Pointing my gun in their direction, I pulled the hammer back. Coop stood beside me with his strap on ready.

"I hope you got my money for the product you using."

The crackhead jumped up and wiped her nose with the back of her hand. She looked me in the eyes, right before I put a single bullet in between them. Her body tumbled forward and hit the floor.

Tone slowly raised his head and his eyes were rolling. White powder was on the rim of his nose. "Ohh shit, Brick. Why you killed her like that?"

"'Oh shit, Brick,' is right. Where the fuck is my money?" I stepped closer to him and pressed the barrel against his forehead.

"It's right there in the bag." He pointed towards the sofa.

"Coop, grab that bag and check it."

Coop picked it up off the floor and moved it up and down, like he was lifting weights. "This shit feels awfully light."

Tone had his hands up in defense mode. "I'm getting rid of the rest tomorrow. I promise I'll have it all then. Brick, I swear."

"Nah, yo' time is up. When you came in this shit, I warned you there were two things I didn't play about. What were they?"

"Your family and money."

"And what did you fuck with?" I asked, with a menacing grin on my face.

"Your money."

"Exactly. Now it's lights out, muthafucka." I dumped two slugs in his chest.

Boca! Boca!

I looked back at Coop and tucked my piece inside the hem of my waistband. "Let's ride, my nigga."

Chapter 8

Zuri

My luxurious vacation had come to an end and I was back in sunny South Florida. The trip was nothing short of amazing and I was ready to get home to my man. Five days with no dick was beyond insane at this point. I couldn't wait to suck and fuck him properly. I mean, eat the dick whole. It needed to hit the back of my throat, boxing with my tonsils. These damn hormones were raging out of control, as usual. My legs rocked like crazy, thinking about his fine ass.

Brick told me to call him when I landed, but I wanted to surprise him. While I was in Cali, I bought a sexy, lace lingerie set. That was my way of thanking him for the wonderful trip and reuniting me with my sister. For that, I would be forever grateful. I also picked us up a matching set of red bottoms. The Uber driver kept looking at me in the rearview mirror and it was bugging the fuck out of my soul, so of course I had to check him.

"Excuse me."

He was cheesing hard like I was asking for his number. "Yes, baby?" His Creole accent was thick.

"Okay, first off, I'm not your baby and two, I need you to keep your eyes on the road." My neck rolled as I got him together real quick.

Looking out the corner of his eye, he acted as if he didn't know what I was talking about. "What do you mean?"

"You watching me more than the road and I want to make it home in one piece. So, I'm gone need you to get that together, because if you crash this car, I will be suing you and I promise you that."

"Calm down, baby. I got you." He smiled and kept driving.

The longest twenty-five minutes of my life were riding in the back of that damn Uber and I was happy it came to an end. He pulled into my driveway and got out to help me with my luggage.

It was a huge relief to see my baby's car was present. I was grateful to say the least, so I gave him a ten-dollar tip and went inside the house, leaving my belongings at the door. I rushed up the stairs, I scurried down the hallway until I made it to the room door. Brick was sitting on the bed smoking a blunt, but I rushed him anyway.

"Baby, I missed you so much." I threw my arms around his neck and kissed him all over his face.

"I missed you too. Why didn't you call me when you landed?" He sat the blunt in the ashtray.

"I wanted to surprise you."

"Oh."

That was not the welcome I was looking for after being gone for almost a full week. "Well, that was dry. I guess you not happy to see me, or you didn't miss me as much as I missed you." I turned on my heels to walk away, but he grabbed my hand, causing me to stand in place.

"Baby, I'm sorry. It's not you. I'm happy to see you, but I'm going through some shit right now."

The emotion was thick in his voice and that wasn't like him. He was always hard, undeniably sexy, but hard as they came. Whatever it was had to be serious and I turned around to give my baby my undivided attention.

"What's wrong?" I asked with great concern.

Brick squeezed my hand and took a deep breath. The gloominess in his eyes told me more than business was on his mind and my first thought was Gucci. Maybe he died and that meant Mehzani was going to need me, just like I needed her in Cali.

"Breanna was hit by a car and she's in stable condition."

That broke my heart instantly and I couldn't do anything but cradle his head in my arms. "I'm so sorry, baby. Why didn't you call me? I would've come back early to be by your side. This isn't something you face alone, baby. It's me and you, remember that."

He held me tight around my waist and sobbed. It was heartbreaking to see him break down and cry. That alone made me love him more than I did, less than a minute ago. I knew how he felt about his daughter, so I understood his pain.

"Let it all out, baby. I'm here now and we're going to get through this together. I promise you won't have to face this alone."

As I held him, my own emotions kicked in and a flow of tears escaped my eyes, falling onto him. Brick was my whole world and if he cried, I would too. If he was hurting, so was I. I believed that we came into each other's lives for a reason. We cried together for a while and when he finally stopped, he leaned up and looked me in the eyes.

"Look at me crying in front of you." He wiped his eyes. "Now I feel all weak and shit," he chuckled.

"That doesn't make you weak. I still see you as a strong black man. Society has made it seem like men can't show emotion, but that's false. It's natural to do so, especially when you love someone."

"I know, but a nigga still feel weak."

"Don't feel weak, baby. I know you're not."

He was silent for a minute before he continued. "I have something to ask you."

"Okay." I sat down beside him and grabbed his hand. "What is it?"

"When she gets out the hospital, I want her to live with me. But, you know I'm going to need some help. I—"

I knew what he was getting at so I cut him off. "Of course I would help you. That's not even a question. She's the best part of you and I love her just as much as I love you. You have my undying support."

"Damn," he sighed. "What would I do without you?

"You'd be miserable, baby." I joked, trying to lighten the mood.

"I don't doubt that shit. My life is fucked up right now."

"I have a question for you." I tilted my head to the side. "Why aren't you up there with her?"

"Well, I thought I was picking you up. So, I didn't want to go up there and then have to leave."

"Well, let's go, because I want to see her."

"Okay. Do you need to change? Or you going like that?" He looked at my relaxed fit and slides as I stood up.

"I'm going like this. What's wrong with it?"

"Nothing. You look cute to me. I'm just asking, since that's what you wore on the plane."

"Oh okay, because I was about to say I look good, thank you."

"I agree. Now come on."

***

Brick and I held hands as we strolled down the hallway of the pediatric wing of the hospital in silence. It was cold as hell in the building and I was glad I opted to keep on my Adidas sweat pants. We moved quickly past the nurse's station en route to Breanna's room. The closer we got, the harder my heart beat in my chest. I didn't know what to expect and that made me nervous. However, I knew I needed to keep my composure, just in case Brick had another episode. I had to be strong for him. Seeing your child in that condition had to be hard on every level and I was empathetic to his needs. He stopped in front of the door and allowed me to walk in first. My first glimpse was of two females sitting comfortably beside Breanna, like they belonged there. They immediately looked up when I stepped in the room. So being the person I am, I spoke since I was the one that entered the room.

"Hello."

"Hi." To my surprise, they both said it back. It was a little dry and so were their facial expressions. But, that suddenly changed when Brick came into the room.

"Hey. I didn't know y'all was up here." Brick walked over to the women and gave them a hug.

The youngest one held him a little too long. "You know I had to come see my sister."

My head snapped back instantly because her response caught me off guard. I stepped in a little closer to see what was really going on, because I know damn well he didn't have another child and failed to tell me about it. If he forgot to mention that, we were definitely going to have a problem when we left. Brick looked up and observed my unit.

"Oh, my bad y'all, this is my lady, Zuri. Zuri, this is my god-daughter, Janae and her mother, Shan."

Brick just don't know he escaped some major issues with me. "Nice to meet you," Shan replied.

"Likewise," I responded.

I left them to talk and walked up to Breanna's bed. Seeing her bruised and broken made me want to break down and cry right there. The way she was messed up really hurt my heart. I was so used to the jazzy little girl, smiling and asking a million questions. Gently, I placed my hand on her arm and rubbed my thumb across her skin. Being up close and personal, I could honestly say I felt his pain. Breanna was like a daughter to me and I loved her. This was my baby's sister lying here and I couldn't picture her not being around anymore. Brick was hopeful about her situation and so was I. As I continued to stare at her, I couldn't help but to lean down and kiss her.

"You have to fight, baby. What would I do if I couldn't see your beautiful face every day?" I leaned down and kissed her forehead carefully, so I didn't touch her stitches. "I hate to see you like this, princess, and so does your dad."

Unable to keep my composure, I started to cry and the tears tumbled fast down my cheeks. I didn't bother wiping them either. Brick stood beside me and put his arm around me. I turned to face him and buried my head in his chest.

"She gone pull through. My baby gone be strong for Daddy."

"I'm praying she does," I replied sincerely.

***

Mehzani

While I was away, Gucci remained on my mind heavily, so I was hopeful that something changed while I was gone. Unfortunately, his condition was worse than I thought. Upon my arrival, the nurse told me he was paralyzed from the waist down. His L-2 vertebra was shattered and pieces were embedded in his spinal cord. That really crushed my heart. To hear he may never walk again was mind boggling, but at least he would survive. That meant a long and painful road was going to be ahead of us. I sat beside his bed and cried my eyes out. The only sound that could be heard was the constant beeping from the monitor and my sniffles. This couldn't be life right now. He was my heart and soul and I couldn't see myself without him. All of my dreams had suddenly become nightmares and I knew nothing would be the same. Life had a fucked-up way at throwing a monkey wrench in my plans. Out of all the men I'd encountered, the good one had to pay an ugly price for the life he chose. The good news was that he was going to pull through, but that was half the battle.

All of that crying was giving me a headache, so I left the room to go to the nurse's station to get something for the pain. Thankfully, his nurse was sitting there.

"Excuse me. Can I get a Tylenol for myself please?" I placed both hands on the counter and waited for her response.

"What's wrong?" Nurse Jackson asked.

"I've cried until I gave myself a headache."

She stood up and opened a drawer, pulling out a tiny white packet. Then, she walked in the direction of where I was standing. "Here you go."

"Thank you."

"You're welcome."

On my way down the hall, I tore the wrapper open, dumped both pills into my hand and balled up the packet. I had bottled water in the room with me. When I walked into the room, I tossed the pills in my mouth and went for my water. Taking a huge gulp, I tossed my head back to swallow them. As I brought my head down, a set of eyes were on me. It frightened me. The bottle and wrapper I was holding slipped from my grip and hit the floor. The water splashed on my feet, but I ignored it.

"Gucci, baby, you're awake." I jumped up and placed both hands on his face. My excitement was hard to contain, but I had to remember he was in a lot of pain and it was probably in his best interest not to touch him. "I thought I lost you. I thought you were going to die. Baby, I'm so happy right now, I could cry."

My mouth rambled one hundred miles a minute. I was so caught up, I never realized he hadn't responded to me. "What happened to you? Who did this to you?"

Gucci looked like he was out of it. All he did was study my face with a blank stare. It seemed as if he recognized me, but I couldn't be so sure about that. I needed him to say something, but he wasn't, and it was frightening. "Baby, I'll be right back. I'm going to get the nurse."

The second I turned on my heels, I froze. Quickly turning back to face him, I remembered I could buzz the nurse from the bed, so that's what I did instead of leaving him alone in that room. It didn't take long for the nurse to enter the room.

"Hey." She strolled in with a slight smile on her face. Since he'd been in the hospital, she'd become very familiar with me. The nurse caught a glimpse of Gucci and her smile widened. "Dear God, he's awake."

"He's awake, but he's not talking. What's going on?" The situation alone was causing me to panic. Especially since his wasn't the recovery I was thinking about.

The nurse checked his eyes, ears and throat. "If you can hear me, blink your eyes twice."

Gucci blinked twice, but his lips never moved. "Can you talk to me? If you can, say hello, if not blink once."

Gucci moved his mouth, but no words were spoken. All we heard were babbling noises. Frustrated, he blinked several times while hitting the bed, and I damn near fell out. I held onto the bed and took a deep breath. "What's happening to him?"

The nurse looked at me, but she appeared to be sad suddenly. "I'm sorry, but he won't be able to speak. He had four strokes while he was in a coma and that has affected his speech tremendously. He's going to need extensive rehab."

"How am I..." Gucci's eyes were on me, so I stopped talking immediately. He was already in bad shape and I didn't want my comment to make him feel worse than he already did. And, I certainly didn't want him to think I was going to turn my back on him. My mind was in a frenzy, thinking about how I could possibly help him recover, if I was unable to communicate with him. Technically, he was a mute and that would make my job harder than I imagined. Our line of communication had been shut off before it could begin. There was no way possible I could do this alone. For certain, I was going to need my sister's help with this.

Chapter 9

Brick

Before my daughter was born, I made a promise I would always protect her and keep her out of harm's way. The five years I was away, there wasn't much I could do, but now that I was home it wasn't shit that could hold me back. That was the reason why I was sitting inside the lawyer's office, prepared to hire her if she was speaking my language.

"So, you want to fight for full custody of your daughter?" Attorney Michelle Coleman rocked back and forth in her seat.

"That's correct. I need my daughter the same way I need oxygen to live. The same way the universe needs gravity." I chose her because I heard she was a beast in the courtroom.

"Okay. Well, before I decide to take the case, I have to make sure it's solid and we have a shot at winning. This is an uphill battle and many attorneys have failed with this type of case. I'm going to be honest with you though, you have to prove the mother is unfit, incapable of taking care of the child, on drugs, unstable or that the child is in danger. In the state of Florida, full custody really doesn't exist, unless the circumstances call for it. Now, what is guaranteed is shared custody."

That wasn't what I wanted to hear, so I cut her off. "No. I want full custody of my daughter. She is in intensive care because of her mother, and I will not lose my child behind her negligence."

Ms. Coleman stopped rocking and grabbed her pen and paper. "What happened?"

"She was hit by a car because her mother wasn't watching her. From my understanding, she was in the house and my daughter was outside alone, looking for me. Hoping I would pick her up." I had to pause and catch my breath. "That's my fault because something kept telling me to pick her up, but I was a day late and a dollar short."

Just talking about the incident had me ready to do something foul. Tears wanted to build up, but I couldn't break. Breanna needed me to be strong and fight for her, so I thought about a happy ending with the two of us and pushed the negative thoughts out my head.

"You weren't there, so it isn't your fault. She was responsible for the safety of your daughter and she failed at doing so. Are there any other incidents that occurred on her watch?"

"None that I know of," I answered truthfully.

"Okay. Now the judge is going to ask if you have legitimate income and a place for her to live. Do you have that?"

"Yes, I do."

"Okay. You will have to show proof of income and residency."

"I have my own business, but I can do that."

"Okay. Great."

"That's all I need?"

"Yes and four thousand dollars," she replied.

"I got that too."

"The retainer is fifteen hundred and I'll get started."

The price was cheaper than I thought, so I dug inside my pocket and peeled off enough hundreds to foot the bill. Attorney Coleman counted the bills and wrote up a receipt.

"I'm going to get started on this right away. I'll keep you updated on every little detail."

"Thank you."

"You're welcome."

I stood up and left her office in a hurry. There were a few more errands I needed to run, before I headed up to see my baby girl.

After I left the lawyer's office, I took a trip to the bank, jewelry store, and health department to get Breanna's birth certificate. My very last stop was to Walmart and I was tired as fuck. All I wanted to do was get in the house and kick my feet up with my lady. Wally World was on swole. It had to be food stamp time because every chick I walked past had a buggy full of food. That shit was overflowing. One chick had two damn buggies, with five kids running behind her. I made my way to the back of the store to the outdoor department. The dude behind the glass counter seemed like he was waiting on a customer to come through.

"Good afternoon. Can I help you find something?"

I placed my keys on the counter and took a deep breath. "Yeah, I need to get a fishing license."

"Oh yeah, I can definitely help you with that. Um. What type of license do you want, freshwater or saltwater?"

"Freshwater."

"Okay. Now I just need your driver's license." Reaching into my back pocket, I retrieved my wallet and took out my license. He reached out for it and I placed it in his hand.

"Is this your current address?"

"Yes."

"The license is going to be forty dollars."

The process took less than thirty minutes and I was out the door to carry on with my day. Finally, I could get home and lay my ass down. The second I walked outside, the rays from the sun kissed me on the back of my neck. Instantly, I could feel sweat roll down the center of my back. So, I picked up the pace and speed-walked to my car. My ass couldn't jump in my whip any faster, before I put the air on full blast. After I cooled off, I put the car in drive and pulled off, so I could take my black ass in the house.

***

Zuri

"Calm down and tell me what's going on, because I can't understand you." When I answered Mehzani's call, I knew something was wrong as soon as she opened her mouth. Immediately, I went back into Brick's bedroom to talk to her.

"It's Gucci," she sobbed. "I don't know what I'm going to do."

That was the moment my heart plummeted to the pit of my stomach. My breathing became shallow all of a sudden and my knees grew weak. I held onto the dresser for safety measures. The first thought that came to mind was that he passed away. I didn't want to jump the gun, so I was trying my best to keep my response to myself.

"What's wrong, sis? Talk to me."

"Gucci. He. He's—"

"He's dead?" I blurted out, since she was having a hard time getting her dialogue together.

"No. No." The sobbing grew a little bit louder. "He's paralyzed. Zuri, my baby can't talk or walk."

"Zhani, I'm so sorry to hear that." I paused in order to get my thoughts together. "I know it sounds bad, but at least he's alive." I sympathized with her pain, although I had never experienced that situation firsthand.

"What am I supposed to do, Z? I can't do this. How am I supposed to care for him?"

A few days ago, it was me who needed to be calmed down. Now, it was Mehzani. "Listen to me. The first thing I want you to do is take a deep breath. You cannot think rationally if your mind is all over the place."

Mehzani took several deep breaths like she was in Lamaze classes. After about sixty seconds, the loud breathing came to a halt.

"Okay. Okay. What's next?" she asked.

"I want you to understand something. Being paralyzed is not the end of the world, okay? Death is the end, so be happy he's still alive. Secondly, you said he couldn't talk, why is that?"

"He had four strokes and now he's slurring really bad. He couldn't utter one word to me when I asked him who shot him."

Mehzani was a lot calmer after the breathing exercises. That was a great help, because now I could understand her words, as she explained everything the doctor said. I was so deep in the conversation, I didn't realize Brick was back until he was a few feet away, causing me to jump out my drawers.

"You scared me."

"That must be a good-ass conversation, since you didn't hear me close the door." He cut his eye at me. "I know that better not be a nigga, either."

His ass was a whole mess, but he knew better. He was just talking shit as usual. "I'm on the phone with Mehzani." I moved the phone and placed it on my chest. "Babe, give me a minute. It's about Gucci."

Brick leaned down in front of me and kissed me on my forehead. "You good, baby. Handle your business. Tell sis I said wassup."

"Tell him I said hi." Her reply was a little dry, but that was to be expected.

"She said hey, baby." Brick left the room immediately so I could continue my conversation in private. "Are you okay?"

"I don't have a choice. I'm all he's got." Mehzani sucked her teeth. "Oh yeah and his crazy-ass mammy."

My overly sensitive ass was always ready to cry at the drop of a dime. The entire situation was sad, especially since I knew that she loved him without a doubt. "Sis, you're not alone. You have me and Brick over here. I promise."

"Thanks sis, 'cause God knows I'm going to need it." Mehzani chuckled, but it was far from laughter. Whenever she did that, it only meant one thing. She was nervous.

"You don't have to thank me. I got your back."

"Well, I'm not going to hold you up. Go ahead and tend to your man."

"Are you sure? Because he can wait until we get off the phone." At that moment, she was my greatest concern. It wasn't like Brick needed me anyway.

"It's okay. I just needed to come outside and vent for a little while. Now that's over and I should get back inside and make sure he's okay."

"Call me if you need anything. I don't care how late at night it is or early in the morning. I'm always available for you, so don't hesitate."

"I love you, sis."

"I love you too," I replied.

"I'll talk to you later."

"Okay."

After I hung up the phone, I went to find Brick. At first glance I didn't see him, but once I hit the corner, I spotted him sitting at the dining room table with his instruments he used to roll his blunts. This time he wasn't paying attention because he was so into his craft. I cleared my throat and he raised his head slowly, finally taking his eyes off of his grinder. Every time he looked at me, I noticed how his eyes always had a sparkle in them.

"How are my babies doing?"

The sound of his voice made the baby move and I knew that to be a fact, because he or she hadn't moved all day. "Better, now that you're back and apparently someone is happy, because I finally feel movement." I walked over to him and grabbed his hand. "Feel it."

Brick placed his hand on my stomach and smiled. "My dude kicking hard. This might be my football player."

"Who said it's a boy? It might be a girl." It really didn't matter to me. As long as the baby was healthy, that's all that mattered.

"This Junior right here. Watch what I tell you."

"We'll see." I hated to ruin this moment, but there was something I needed to address. "Umm. I need to ask you a question."

"Okay."

"So, I just got off the phone with Mehzani and she was telling me Gucci woke up today." I watched his facial expression, but it never changed. He remained attentive to what I was saying.

"He's paralyzed and he can't talk. Baby, she's so broken up about this. All she did was cry the entire time we were on the phone." I paused for a minute to see if he would jump in, but all he did was stare deeply into my eyes. "I feel so bad for her."

"So, what's the question?" He moved his hand from my stomach and placed it in his lap.

"Umm." I was trying to find the proper words to speak, but they couldn't be located. "I don't know how to say this."

"Just ask the question."

"Are you responsible for what happened to Gucci?" I blurted out.

The pregnant pause in the room was unsettling and my mind was starting to wonder if I hit the nail on the head. Brick sat back in his seat and folded his arms across his chest. "Why would you ask me that?"

"Because I want to know."

Brick shook his head. "Nah. That ain't why you asked me that. What's the real reason?"

"That is the real reason. Now answer my question. Did you do it?" I placed my hands on my hip. "And don't lie to me."

Brick moved his arms and stood up. His hands were at his side as he approached me. "Zuri, stop playing with me and answer my question. You opened this door and I want an answer."

My eyes were locked into his as I took a step back. "So, you gone hit me because I asked you a question?" I placed my hand on my belly so he wouldn't forget I was carrying our child.

He stopped in his tracks. "Hit you?" he repeated. "You can't be serious. Have I ever hit you before?" The disappointment was thick in his voice like a foreign accent.

"No." I shook my head.

"So, what makes you think I would start now?"

Brick made a valid point, but that didn't make me feel comfortable enough to not ask. "I don't know. I guess because of the way you got up."

"I thought you knew me better than that." I knew he was pissed at me, but then he placed his finger under my chin and gently tilted my head up. Brick kissed me on my lips. "You should know the man you sleeping with a little bit better than you do."

Brick walked off, leaving me in my thoughts. I had to admit I felt a little silly for thinking he was about to hit me. It wasn't like I gave him a reason to do it, unlike Deja. Instead of leaving him alone to collect his thoughts, I walked in the room a few minutes after him. He was lying on his stomach, with his head turned to the wall.

"Baby," I called out, but he didn't respond. "I'm sorry. I didn't mean to upset you." His phone vibrated and rang, but he didn't bother to get up and check it.

Slowly, I walked up to the bed and sat down beside him. The phone started going off again. Whoever it was wanted to talk badly. That wasn't my concern at the moment, so I focused on the situation at hand.

"Truthfully speaking, my sister didn't say anything else to me besides what I told you. And, the reason I asked you was because that night I kept Breanna, you said you were going to straighten him out because of what he did to you. So, now can you see why I asked you that in the first place?"

"Yeah, I hear you," he mumbled. Just then, a notification came through his phone and now I was annoyed.

"Who the fuck keep blowing your phone up? And, why you not answering?"

"Shiidd, I don't know."

Brick never had an issue with me touching his phone, so I picked it up and opened the text message. The image that popped up made my hand tremble terribly. I could feel the tears build up in my eyes. After all this time, I just knew I had a faithful and loyal man. Now it made sense as to why he said I should get to know the man I'm sleeping with. Bold and in my face, was a picture of a female wearing a three-piece, black lace garter set with the caption, *"How do you like this, daddy?"*

My blood was boiling and I wanted to strangle his ass with the bed sheet. Instead of doing that, I hit him in the head with his phone, while screaming, "Who the fuck is this? So, you cheating now?"

Brick rolled over on his stomach with a scowl on his face. "What the fuck is yo' problem? Ain't nobody cheating. Yo' ass trippin'."

"Look in that phone and call me a liar." I stood there with my arms folded, huffing and puffing. He grabbed the phone, but he was too busy looking at me, like I was making the shit up. "I can't believe you out here cheating on me and shit. And while I'm carrying your fucking child at that. You made me quit my job and stop talking to someone who was only a friend."

"Chill the fuck out, 'cause you trippin' about nothing." Brick finally looked down at the phone. I watched him scroll through it and when he was done, he looked up at me. Before he spoke a word, he shook his head and ran his hand across his face. "It's not what you think."

"What the fuck do you mean, 'it's not what I think?' I think you fucking the next bitch. Why else would she be texting you some shit like that?"

The tears that built up in my eyes began to stream down my face rapidly. Just when I thought I met a solid nigga, he turned right around and proved me wrong. I couldn't lie, that shit hurt me to the depth of my soul and I quickly became sick to my stomach.

"I've been faithful and honest with you and you would turn around and do this to me?" My cries turned into loud sobs. "I trusted you."

"Baby, listen to me. I can explain all of this." He started to ease his way out of the bed.

"No, you can't, and I'm leaving."

His feet hit the floor. "Zuri, where are you going?"

"Where I should've been in the first place. Home."

"I'll prove it to you. Just give me a chance." The phone was still in his hand and all of a sudden, it started to ring on speaker. It rang for a while before a female picked up.

"Did you like the picture?" When she said that, I wanted to slap the shit out of him and curse her out, but I remained silent.

"Aye, Sparkle. What did I tell you about showing me shit I don't plan on seeing? This is strictly business and nothing else."

"Shit. My bad, boss. If I would've known you was gone be bent out of shape, I wouldn't have sent it in the first place." The chick on the phone sucked her teeth.

"Yeah, don't send that shit to my phone. I have a wife and I don't need her thinking we fucking."

"It won't happen again." Then, she hung up.

"Happy now?" Brick tossed the phone back on the stand.

"Oh, that was supposed to make me feel better?" I rolled my eyes hard, because I wasn't satisfied. That did not explain why she sent the picture in the first place.

"I just proved to you I'm not fucking that girl."

"That's probably some shit y'all had planned, just in case yo' ass got busted."

"Man, that ho' an escort."

"Are you serious right now? A fucking escort. You could've done better than that." I stormed out of the room, but I could hear his heavy footsteps behind me.

"Zuri, where are you going?"

"Home," I screamed, while heading towards the door. "I'm not doing this shit with you."

"I ain't do shit," he yelled, while grabbing my arm and turning me towards him.

"Don't yell at me because you got caught. This is all your fault, not mine," I yelled back at him.

Chapter 10

Brick

I hated to see her cry and I could understand why she was so upset, but I didn't cheat on her and that was the God's honest truth. So, instead of escalating the problem further, I lowered my voice so we could talk like adults.

"Baby, hear me out." She shook her head no. "Please, Zuri. I swear it's not what you think."

Using my right hand, I placed my thumb underneath her eye and wiped away the tears that were constantly falling. "Stop crying. You know I hate to see you like this. Come in the room and let me explain everything to you."

Taking her hand in mine, I led her back to the bedroom. This was certainly not the way I wanted to bring her up to speed about my business ventures. However, my hands were tied and I didn't have a choice, thanks to Sparkle's silly ass.

"Have a seat." Zuri sat down on the bed, resting both hands on her protruding belly. Her eyes were settled on the carpet. "Look at me."

She shook her head no and sniffled. "I don't want to."

"Baby, please." I lifted her chin so she could look me in my eyes, but she clinched her eyes tightly to avoid all contact.

"I can't stand to look at you right now. So, please just leave me alone." She bit down on her bottom lip.

"Okay, it's like this." I paused to see if she would open them, but when she didn't, I continued. "A few weeks ago, my Cuban connect asked me to find him some girls and he'd pay me fifteen hundred a piece. Coop found me a set of twins and I presented them to my connect. Needless to say, he was happy with the merchandise and shot me a check for thirty bands. That's when I decided to start the escorting business."

Zuri opened her eyes, but her mean mug was still present. "Sounds good and it's very well thought out, if you ask me. But, do you really expect me to believe that?"

"I'm telling you the truth and I'll show you." The check Hector gave me was secured away in Breanna's room, so I walked away to get it. When I returned, she was still in the same exact spot.

Proving my innocence was important to me, because without trust, we had nothing. The minute she stopped trusting me and deemed me a cheater, my business moves would be affected. That was certainly going to result in her constantly calling and texting to make sure I'm not knocking down another bitch. I'm a grown-ass man and I don't need anyone checking up on me. I dropped the bag at her feet and knelt down in front of her.

"Here is the proof."

I unzipped the bag and her eyes lit up. Yet, she was still frowning. "Where did you get all that money from?"

Purposely ignoring her question, I pulled out the manila envelope and handed it to her. "That's the check for thirty grand to start the business. In the duffle bag, that's a hundred grand for me to bring them ten more girls over the next few weeks."

Zuri was finally giving me direct eye contact and her face was no longer balled up. That probably meant she believed me, but I couldn't be sure of that until she expressed that verbally.

"All of this may be true, but that doesn't dismiss the fact that another female is sending my man some fucking nude pictures."

"Okay, okay. You win. What I'm not about to do is continue to argue about something I didn't do. This is the last piece of proof I can give you and if this ain't enough, I don't know what else to say or do."

Hopefully, this last call would make her believe me. I hated tension in my household, because that shit was uncomfortable. That would lead me to not wanting to be home and ultimately, that leads to cheating. And, that was something I wasn't interested in doing. True enough, we weren't married, but I owed it to her to be faithful. With the phone now in my hand, I scrolled through my call log and dialed the number I needed to set me free.

"You're a very smart girl, so all you have to do is be quiet and listen. This conversation will ease your mind." The phone rang a little longer than usual, but I finally got an answer.

"Waddup, bruh?" Coop sounded like he was still in the bed.

"Shit, coolin'. You was sleep?"

"Not yet. My ass was dozing off, tho. Everything cool?" he asked.

"Yeah. I need the number to the realtor, so I can look at some places to set up shop soon."

"I guess that means Zuri is on board with everything." He laughed. "How did you get her to agree to you opening up a damn escorting business?"

"Man," I sighed to make it believable. "I ain't tell her yet. My plan was to do that today, but I need to handle Sparkle ass first."

"What happened?" Coop's voice heightened through the speaker. It looked like Zuri's ears perked up and she tuned in a little harder, like she was waiting to hear some bad shit.

"She crossed the line by sending me nude pics and shit. I told her ass from the jump I don't need to see shit I ain't smashing."

Coop busted out laughing. "Yeah, you did tell her that. Her ass persistent. She asked me about you too. I told her you ain't fuckin' nobody but your girl, so she can get that out her head."

The look on Zuri's face was priceless. She was lucky I couldn't get a picture of her ass looking silly in the face. I knew I was good, so I smiled and blew her a kiss. "Facts. I got my goddess already, so the rest of these ho's dead. I ain't worried about no new pussy. I'm focused on stacking this cash for my family, man."

"I'ma give it to you, bruh, you good 'cause Sparkle been trying to fuck you from day one and you brush her ass off every time. If it was me, I probably would've smashed already."

"Yeah and that's why you having problems now. You need some self-control. Stop letting ya' dick do all thinking for you. That bitch will have you in a jam," I chuckled.

"Nah. I'm using condoms over here. Besides, it's Danielle's fault I moved out. She didn't believe me when I said I wasn't cheating and I got sick of that shit. That muthafucka don't know I been turning down pussy for about eight months now. Fuck it now. I'm outchea."

In my eyes, Zuri heard way more than she needed to hear, so I had to end the call quickly before he started talking some more shit. He already said too damn much. "Aye, bruh, I gotta go. Shoot me that number and remember what I just said."

"Fa'sho."

"A'ight. I'll get at you later." When I hung up the phone, Zuri was standing there with her arms folded. I sat my phone back down and walked up to her. "Do you believe me now?"

"I'm not going to lie. At first, I didn't believe you and I thought it was staged. But, after listening to him talk, I don't believe he would've said half of that shit if he knew I was standing right here."

"You have my word that I'll never cheat on you." Placing my hands on her hips, I pulled her closer to me and laid a sloppy, wet kiss to her mouth. She reciprocated as I knew she would. Zuri pulled the waistband of my joggers and slipped her hand inside my boxers. We continued to kiss aggressively, while she stroked my stiffening dick. She was certainly trying to get some shit started and I wasn't up for stopping her either. Zuri jacked me off until I was hard as the light post outside my window. Her free hand was busy pulling my pants down. Normally, I would stop a female from taking off my pants like I was a little ass boy, but Zuri had a way of making me do shit I wouldn't let slide.

Once she successfully got my joggers down to my knees, she broke our kiss and eased down to the floor. My clothes followed and once they were at my feet, I stepped out of them. Zuri grabbed my dick with her hand and eagerly shoved it into her mouth. Her head moved back and forth rapidly. Then, she pulled it out, spit on it and slurped it back up. My knees grew weak instantly when she used both hands to twist and suck it at the same damn time. I grabbed a handful of her hair and rocked my hips to her beat, giving her complete control of my body. I belonged to her as much she belonged to me.

A few minutes passed and she was still slurping and jacking my dick, turning me on with the sound alone. I knew if she didn't ease up, I would be letting go all of my babies in her mouth, but that wasn't the way I wanted to nut. I loosened the grip I had on her hair and eased backwards so she could stop. Zuri licked her lips, removing the pre-cum that glistened on her lips like lip gloss. I leaned down and kissed her in the mouth, before I helped her to her feet.

"Take all that off," I instructed her to get naked. "And get on the bed. I want you face down, ass up."

Zuri did like she was told and assumed the fucking position. She was submissive and that's what I loved about her. She knew to follow the lead of a real man, one that would never steer her wrong. I walked up from behind and caressed her ass before smacking both cheeks. Slowly, I rubbed her pussy lips, then her clit with my wandering hand. She was certainly hot down there, so I eased two fingers inside her box and pushed them in and out. She was wet as fuck and I wanted a taste of that honey dew. My fingers and tongue switched positions. I took my time licking every inch of her pretty, succulent lips, but I moved a little slower when it was time to suck on her clit. I held it between my lips and I could feel it throbbing in my mouth, as it swelled up and got hard like a jelly bean.

"Ooohh. Stop teasing me and put it in," Zuri purred, while pushing her ass closer to my face.

All that did was warrant me to tongue fuck her. Spreading her cheeks, I ran my tongue down the crack of her ass, right before I spit in it and pushed my thumb inside. Using my tongue, I parted her lips and slithered my way deep down inside her pussy. It was so far in there, I felt like I could touch her uterus. Zuri dropped her head and fucked me back. Her ass cheeks clapped in my face and I kept on fucking her in both holes.

"Oooh. Yes. Yes. Shit. I'm coming." Zuri was moaning and rocking her body and I didn't even drop the dick in yet. My dude was semi-hard, but not rocked up enough. I held him in my hand and pulled on it until he reached his full length. An overflow of juices oozed from her fat melon and my tongue welcomed all of it, every single drop. I clamped down on her clit while she was coming and nibbled on it.

"Fuck. Fuck. Shit. Ahh." Zuri grabbed the sheets and buried her head deeper into the mattress to let out a few screams. She was still coming, so I stopped wasting time and drove my dick deep in them guts.

"Ahh shit," I grunted.

That first stroke always had the ability to take me out. I was a G and it was my duty to tame the cat, but it was something about pregnant pussy that felt so damn good. It started off slow, but I couldn't help myself and I had to put it down.

"Raise up," I demanded. Zuri straightened her back and arms, so that she was only on her knees. "Keep one hand on the bed so you don't fall."

With my stomach pressed against her back, I placed my hand at the base of her neck and choked her just enough to give her pleasure. While I hit it from the back, I bit down on her neck and sucked on it.

"Ah! Ah! Daddy. Shit," she whispered softly.

"You like it, don't you?"

"Yes, baby." Zuri licked her lips.

"Who pussy this is?"

"Yours."

"You sho' 'bout that?" I double-checked.

That question alone made me thrust inside of her harder, with little regards that I was probably disturbing my baby. Fuck that tho', I was his daddy and I was the reason he was in there in the first place.

"Ouuu! Yes. I promise." Zuri wasn't crazy. She knew I would kill her ass if she even thought about giving my pussy up. My hand was already in the right place, and it wouldn't take much to break her neck.

"You better not. I'll kill both of y'all. I promise you that." I ran my tongue up and down her neck. "Understand me?"

"Yes, Daddy." I loved when she called me Daddy. That shit turned me on in the worst way.

"This dick feel good to you?"

"Yes, Daddy."

"It's all yours too. I promise."

"I know."

"Ouuu, I love you so much," I grunted.

"I love you too," Zuri replied.

"Play with that pussy so you can come on this dick again." She moved her hand and when I felt her fingertips graze my balls, I knew she was putting in work down there. That was my cue to dig deeper in that cat from the back. Sweat poured down my face as I humped hard and fast, delivering Grade-A dick. Zuri matched my thrusts blow for blow until I shot hot, white snot against her vaginal walls.

After an amazing round of sex, we were sprawled across the bed, recouping in silence. My hand was resting on her stomach, as my mind drifted off to Breanna. I was ready for my baby to open her eyes and acknowledge me so I could take her home with me and nurse her back to health. My promise was still in effect and I was standing on that. No one would have the ability to hurt her again. The sound of Zuri clearing her throat caught my attention.

"Bae," she whispered softly.

"Yeah."

"We have an honest relationship, right? No secrets."

"Yes," I replied smoothly. It was the truth, but I wasn't sure what her questions were leading up to. "What's on your mind?"

"I'm curious to know why you didn't feel the need to tell me about the escorting services you been providing. Like, what are you hiding?"

"I'm not hiding anything from you and I was going to tell you. But, with everything that was going on, I decided to put it off until I had everything in order."

"I get that, but I don't want to feel like I can't trust you," she sighed. "Then, that picture made it worse. I doubted you and I don't like feeling that way. What if the shoe was on the other foot? And, we both know how you feel about secrets."

Since I was a real man, I understood exactly where she was coming from and for that I couldn't be upset. "You right. I apologize for not telling you sooner, but it was for a good reason though."

"Yeah, we'll see about that." Her ass didn't sound too convincing.

"I just showed and proved to you that I'm not lying about nothing. So I don't know what else to tell you."

"We can start off by you telling the truth at all times and reiterating to that ho', you off limits."

"I can hold my own and I can certainly handle a female throwing pussy at me. It ain't the first time. Besides, I'm a grown-ass man and I'm beyond giving my dick the power to ruin my damn relationship. You're all I want and you need to realize that."

The fact she was still doubting me with her huffing and puffing was irritating as hell. She better believe that if I was cheating she would feel it. I had the ability to cave her heart deep into her chest cavity. But, to keep things from escalating any further, I knew what needed to be done. There was no other way around it.

"Alright. I can already see where this is going." Slowly, I eased from underneath her and sat upright in the bed. Leaning forward, I picked up my boxers from the floor. "Let's just gone 'head and put it out there."

When I turned to face Zuri, she appeared to be confused, being that I hadn't fully disclosed any information. "What do you mean?"

"Sit tight. I'm about to show you."

When I first made it back to my place, I left the documents on the table, so I went into the living room to retrieve the envelope. Zuri was sitting with her back against the headboard, covered with the blanket. Her hands were folded in her lap and her feet were crossed at the ankles. I guess she wanted to be comfortable for everything I was about to drop on her.

"So, it's like this." I took a deep breath, because I knew she wasn't going to take majority of my news well. "Somebody is targeting me. I don't know who or why. All I know is that those bullets were intended for me for the simple fact that I saw that truck before by your house. So, with that being said, you can't stay there until I figure out who's behind it."

Zuri's eyes stretched wide and she gasped, while placing her hand on her chest. "What? Are you serious?"

I nodded my head. It was partially the truth. I couldn't tell her that a tracker was found in my car. Out of fear that I didn't know how she would respond and plus, I needed her to know I would die keeping her safe. "You can't leave my place under any circumstances. Not unless I'm with you or I have someone to be your security."

"So, in other words, I have to be babysat?"

"Don't fight with me on this. It's not safe for you or my babies right now. I'm looking into getting a house, so be patient with me." I sat down on the bed, but my eyes were still on her. "Do you understand what I'm telling you?"

A few seconds passed before she replied, "Yes. I'll do whatever you want me to do."

"Thank you." I opened up the envelope, pulled out the paperwork from the lawyer and handed it to her. "That's all I ask."

"What's this?" Zuri eyed the documents in her hand.

"I filed for full custody of Breanna." It hurt my chest to allow the next words flow from my lips. "In the event something happens to me, I want you to promise me you will take care of my babies and not just the one you carrying. Breanna too."

Zuri raised her head slowly with tears in her eyes. "You know I will, but I can't imagine life without you. What am I supposed to do? And, what about Deja?"

That shit hurt to see her like that, but I had to remain strong. With everything that was going on, there was no telling what might happen. I just needed her to be prepared for the worst.

"Zuri, baby." Taking her hand into mine, I kissed her fingertips. "This is not the time for you to get soft on me. I need a rider. Somebody that's gone hold me down and ride with me. And, don't worry about Deja. I'll take care of that."

"Okay," she used her free hand to wipe her tears. "I can do that for you. Just tell me what I need to do."

"That's what I need to hear." Her willingness made me smile. There was a lot of work to be done, but I knew she could be trained over time.

Chapter 11

Zuri

Brick was my whole world and the best thing to ever happen to me, so to hear that he could possibly be killed wasn't sitting well with me, point-blank period. All I wanted to do was cry, but I promised him I would be strong and that was what I was prepared to do. I'll be damned if I lose him and fuck up the chance for us to start our family.

"So, what's the plan, because losing you isn't an option?" My ears were perked up so I could take it all in. I wasn't a shooter, but I beat ass. However, I knew this was going to take me to the next level.

"I know this is going to be hard for you to digest, but I need you on your A-game with this. Sadly, this is the life I chose and now you're involved and I don't like it no more than you do."

Brick picked up the bag from the floor and sat it on the bed. I watched closely as he rambled through the contents. A few seconds later, he pulled out a small cellphone. "Take this phone and if it ever rings, that means one thing." He hesitated and shook his head. "It means I'm dead."

Brick passed me the phone and I took it. My fingers trembled because now I feared the worst. He grabbed my hand and held it tightly in his.

"Zuri, if that phone rings, you won't have time to mourn my death. You will need to get out of town and fast. Grab Breanna, go to the bank and remove everything from that deposit box. That is your ticket to get out of here. Do not look back. You will have enough money to start over. Once you get to where you going, you can take all the time you need to mourn me."

"What?" I shook my head rapidly from side to side in disagreement. "No. No. Hell no." She hit the mattress with her fist. "So that means I can't bury you either? I don't like this shit at all, Brick. How the hell we supposed to visit you and bring flowers?"

Zuri closed her eyes and grunted. "Ugh. Why do I have to go through this with you? It's like I'm planning your damn funeral in advance. That's not the life I planned for us."

"I know baby and death is my last option. I will do everything I can to come back to you and my babies. It's not like I plan on dying or no shit like that. It's just that I don't know what to expect in these streets, since I don't know who's behind it. But, just in case, you can have a proper burial for me. All you have to do is have my body flown to you, so you can have a private memorial. It's a simple solution. I wanted to be buried next to my mom and dad, but for you, I'll go wherever you go."

Zuri's eyes shot open. "I don't care how charming you are or how sweet you make it sound. I still don't like it. Why can't we just get out of here and go start over?"

"None of this is guaranteed. Hell, everything may work out as planned. This is just a safety measure I need you to take." He looked in my eyes and spoke with so much conviction. "And besides I don't run from wars, fights, none of that shit. Watch I be the last man standing."

Brick sighed and stuck his hand back inside the bag. "On a happier note, this is what I want you to do."

My attitude was on one thousand. With my arms folded, I let out a long sigh. "There is no happy note."

He smile and passed me the check he showed me earlier. "I'm going to have someone escort you around town. It will probably be Coop or Skeet, because I don't trust anyone else to protect you."

I took the check from his hand. "And, what am I supposed to do with this?"

"Find the office space, so we can open up the escort service. We need to open some legit businesses to make sure I can get Breanna and to make sure you straight. I have the rim shop, but we need more."

All I heard was escort service and my ears started to burn. I held the check up in the air. "Do you really think I want you to start a full-fledged fuckin' escort business? Hell no. That's not gone work for me. Make me think you trying to send me to prison or some shit."

Brick laughed and shook his head. "Chill out. I'm not running that shit, you are. I'll assist you, but you will solely deal with the girls. They won't even have my phone number."

He could be so damn convincing that it got on my nerves, but I couldn't give in so easily. "I don't know about that."

"Yes, you do. You see this one hundred grand in this bag? All of that is for ten girls. That thirty-thousand-dollar check you holding was for a weekend with two girls. So, don't tell me you can't do it. These some high rollers and they willing to pay. All you have to do is round up some bad ass females and get paid."

Now I had to admit, the escort service sounded like a very lucrative business and making that much money was something I never saw in my future. At least not working at my last job. After thinking it over for a brief moment, I had my answer.

"Okay. I'll do it," I agreed.

"Good. Take that check to the bank and open a business account. You need a name, so think about it. Remember, this is all you and I will set up a meeting with Sparkle and Starr, to inform them of the changes."

"Not by yourself you ain't," I snapped.

"Nah, this meeting is for the boss and that's you. I'll introduce y'all and we'll go from there."

"Okay."

"Once everything is rolling and we have verifiable income, I'll start depositing the drug money into the business account. We can't sleep in the house with the money."

"I got it. My da..." I paused to keep myself referring to Daman as my daddy. "I mean, Daman, used to sell dope when I was younger, so I've been exposed to the game."

By the look on Brick's face, I could tell that was one person he didn't care to speak on. Just the mention of his name made him give me the side eye, so I quickly changed the subject. "So, what area do you want me to find a spot?"

"Anywhere but the hood. We need a spot with the least police activity, so do your research and when you ready to start looking, let me know so I can make the arrangements."

"Okay."

In my mind, I immediately thought about Javier. It had been a while since I'd been up to his shop to get a massage. It looked like I would be paying him a visit soon. Then, I thought about Jason, but I already knew that wouldn't be a good idea although I missed our friendship.

Brick's phone rang and that immediately snapped me out of my thoughts. "Hello." In silence, I sat and watched his facial expressions to see if I could figure out who he was talking to. "Yes, this is Mr. Riccardo."

He was silent for a few moments, as he looked off staring at nothing in particular. More words were spoken and whatever it was had to be good news, because the crease in his mouth moved upward into a smile. "That's great news, Doc. I'm coming down now."

A smile spread across my lips as well, because that meant Breanna was doing well. My focus remained on Brick. "Okay. I'll be there in one hour. Thank you."

Brick hung the phone up and threw his phone onto the floor. I hadn't seen him that happy in a while. He caught me off guard when he jumped onto the bed, hovering over my body and shouting, "My baby woke and she can finally come home."

"That's great news, baby." I was ecstatic.

"I know." Brick kissed me all over my face. "I know. I know and I'm so damn happy."

A giggle escaped my lips. "I know and I'm happy too. We need to get her something."

"I bought her a necklace when I was out earlier," he replied.

"Without me?" I smacked his arm. "You real nasty for that."

Brick straddled my legs and rubbed my stomach. "Yep and we have one hour to be nasty before our alone time comes to an end. When she gets here, she'll have all of our attention."

"I agree, so stop wasting time." Brick stepped from the bed and removed his boxers once again.

Anxiously anticipating my man to stroke me into a semi-coma, I moved the blanket off my body and exposed my naked frame. My hand made a trail from my nipples all the way down to my vagina. Brick watched in amazement, as I rubbed my clit and licked my lips. Unable to just stand there and not do anything, he climbed into bed, ready to put in work. My legs were wide open, awaiting his nose dive into the motherland.

***

Mehzani

Today was the happiest day of my life. The hospital had called two days ago and said Gucci would be coming home today. I was mixed with every emotion you could think of happy, sad, joy and pain. The guilt of sleeping with Mel was starting to weigh on me heavy like an anchor. I wanted to tell him, but I was afraid he would leave me. But, at the same time, I didn't want to keep any secrets from him. I loved him with everything in me and I would do anything to keep him.

The pounding coming from the front door rattled my sinful thoughts from my mind. "Ugh," I sighed heavily and rolled my eyes, because I already knew who it was. "Speaking of the devil."

With no sense of urgency, I slid off the sofa and stuck my feet into my house shoes. Mel knocked a little more aggressively, but that wasn't going to make me run. "I'm coming," I shouted, using my vocals.

When I finally made it to the door, Mel was standing there with his hands in his pockets. The way he was biting down on his lip gave me the impression that he was nervous or concerned about something.

"Hello. Are you just going to stand there in silence?" While I awaited his answer, I leaned against the door frame with my arms folded.

Mel looked up at me, finally opening his mouth. "I'm sorry. I have a lot on my mind. Can I come in?"

"Sure." I took a step back, so he could walk in.

"I haven't seen you since you been back from your trip. How are you?" He walked over to the sofa and sat down in the very spot we had sex.

"I'm good." Instead of sitting beside him, I took a seat in the chair adjacent to the sofa.

"You sure about that?"

"I'm fine."

Mel leaned forward with his hands folded and elbows resting on his knees. "So, you wasn't going to tell me Gucci was coming home today?"

That took me by surprise, but I kept my poker face intact. "They actually called me earlier today. So, I'm still processing it all. Is that why you came over here?"

"Yes and no."

"That's not a straight answer, so why are you really here?" Trick questions weren't my thing and I needed him to give me a solid answer. "And how did you know he was coming home today?"

"Honestly," he sighed. "I called up there to check on him and that's when they told me he would be discharged today. So, once I found out, I figured I should come over and talk to you about us."

Before I knew it, my head snapped back and my lips were tooted up to the max like I could smell shit lingering in the air. "Us? There is no us. I'm sorry, but that night was a mistake. I love Gucci."

"So, you don't think we should tell him what happened between us?" His eyes drifted in the opposite direction, breaking our eye contact.

"Huh?" I asked, just to be sure I heard him correctly.

Mel continued to look at nothing in particular. "I was asking if you think we should tell Gucci about what happened between us."

Truthfully speaking, I wasn't prepared to do that. Nor was I sure if I ever wanted to reveal another weak moment of mine. Then, I remembered the incident with Deja, and how he promised to be honest with me going forward. Gucci had his one indiscretion and now I had mine. He wasn't going to have a choice but to forgive me. The same way I forgave him. Our situations weren't any different.

"I want to, but I don't think this is a good time. He's been through a lot already and he doesn't need any extra stress. We have a long road ahead of us. Not to mention, he can't speak."

Mel scratched his head and took a deep breath. I wasn't a fool and I could sense the dismay in his voice. "So, we should keep quiet?"

"We need to at least wait until he comes home first and then we can sit down and tell him together. I believe that's the best way."

"Alright ma that's on you, but I think we should tell him. I have never betrayed him like this and the shit don't feel right."

"I know, but what if he leaves me?" Now I was nervous.

"I doubt he would, but you have to give him a chance to make that decision. We made this bed and now we have to lay in it. I feel fucked up about what happened. I'm just worried about where we go from here."

"I'll take the blame since it's my fault anyway. I crossed that line, so I'll deal with the consequences."

"I could've stopped you, but I gave in too easily. So, I'm to blame as well." Mel sat upright and looked me in the eyes. "How about we see what his state of mind is, and then we will just go from there? Is that a deal?"

"Yes."

Mel stood up and walked over to where I was sitting. When he placed his hand on my shoulder, I flinched. "Relax. Everything is going to work itself out. Let's go and pick him up."

On our way to the hospital, our conversation was non-existent. During the entire ride, I stared out the window in heavy thought. The radio was low, so apparently, Mel wasn't interested in listening to music. So I connected the aux cord to my phone and found a song that spoke to my soul, revealing how I was feeling. I turned up the volume on the stereo, as he focused back on the traffic in front of us.

I sang the lyrics to Nicki Minaj's song, "Right Thru Me," silently.

You see right through me. How do you do that shit How do you do that shit. How do you do that shit How do you, how do you, how do you, how do you, how do you. You let me win. You let me ride. You let me rock. You let me slide. And when they lookin' you let me hide. Defend my honor, protect my pride. The good advice I always hated. But looking back, it made me greater.

As I rapped along, tears streamed down my face. Everything about that song was in relation to what Gucci did for me. The way he defended me when ho's tried to attack my character and the way he made me a stronger woman. That was the woman he needed at the moment. But, of course, I had to betray his trust by sleeping with his best friend and right-hand man. God was my witness, I felt like the dirtiest ho' walking the streets. How was I supposed to explain my actions during a vulnerable moment? A painful time where I thought he wasn't going to live.

By the time the song was over, we made it to our destination. As soon as I stepped from the car, I could feel my palms getting sweaty. I was nervous and anxious at the same time. I had this weird feeling Gucci would see right through me like he was psychic. Just like the song. I knew I probably wouldn't be able to keep this secret for long, thanks to the guilt kicking my ass.

"Chill out, ma. You look guilty as hell." Mel smirked and led the way.

"Yeah, that's easy for you to say," I mumbled and followed behind him, taking baby steps all the way to the check-in desk, then to Gucci's room.

Mel walked with a bounce. Clearly showing signs he wasn't fazed by our little indiscretion. Suddenly, that all faded when he stepped foot in the room. He quickly turned on his heels and grabbed my shoulders.

I gaped in confusion. "What's wrong with you?"

"Before you walk in there, I need you to remain calm." He glanced quickly behind him, then back at me.

"For what?" I pulled away from him and rushed into the room. The minute I saw what he was referring to, I snapped. "Ho', what the fuck you doing in here?"

Deja stood up and looked me up and down, like I was in the wrong place or the mistress for that matter. "What the fuck does it look like? I'm visiting." That stank ho' had the nerve to roll her neck.

"It look like you want your ass beat the fuck up." I attempted to rush towards her, but Mel grabbed me. She was talking mighty reckless, like she never heard about me. True enough, she heard I was on flakka, but I also knew she heard these hands were up to date. Whatever she was thinking, she had me fucked up and I was about to show her as soon as I got this nigga up off of me.

"Come on, ma, chill. You can't do that in here."

"Bruh, let me go." I used my strength to try and break free, but he was stronger than a muthafucka.

He looked at Deja in utter disgust. "Real talk, man, what you doing here? You know damn well bruh wouldn't let this shit go down like this."

"Boy, bye." She flicked him off and laughed. "You know what it is, just like he do."

"I'm telling you now get the fuck up outta here befo' I let her go. I'm tryna spare you the embarrassment." Mel pushed me towards the bed to give her some space to walk through. Deja was lucky she left when she did because she was two seconds from getting knocked clean out her muthafuckin' shoes.

The whole time I was arguing, I never looked at Gucci until that very moment and I swear, I wanted to slap the spit from his mouth just because she was there. "Why the fuck you got this ho' in here?"

Gucci's eyes were stretched wide as he shook his head rapidly from side to side. I didn't know what any of that meant, but I knew it was a sign of frustration. He looked at Mel with sadness in his eyes.

"Mehzani," Mel shouted. "Stop. Don't do that. You know what he going through and you know damn well she came up here on her own. I made the bitch leave, so just chill."

"Yeah, whatever. That ho' ain't just popping up out the blue for nothing and he know that shit." I took a seat in the chair next to the bed and crossed my legs, while pouting. "And you know that shit too."

"Ion know what you talkin' about."

"Sure you don't, but anyway, can you go to the nurse's station and let them know we ready to go?"

"Yeah," he replied.

As soon as Mel walked out the room, I got up from the seat and stood next to Gucci. "You must think I'm stupid. This girl is not popping up for no damn reason and as soon as you can talk, you better tell me what I need to know. I'm telling you now, if I find out you've been hiding something from me, I'm leaving you after I get you well and that's a promise."

Gucci's stare was blank and his eyes were glassy. It seemed like my woman's intuition was correct and there was something he was hiding from me. My heart began to race, because I didn't have a clue about what was up and there was no telling when he would be able to tell me. Since I was a very inquisitive person, I couldn't let it rest. I was determined to get an answer.

"Is there something you've been keeping from me? Blink once for yes."

The anticipation was killing me as I waited for a response. Gucci was my whole world and I couldn't picture him not being in it, especially after his near-death experience. All I wanted to do was take my baby home and get him back to his old self. I watched closely as the tears streamed down the side of his face. He then blinked his eyes once and my heart dropped to the pit of my stomach.

"Were you still sleeping with her before the shooting?" Gucci shook his head no and that had me confused at what the secret could be. I was relieved just a little, but I still needed to know what the hell he had to tell me.

Chapter 12

Daman

Steve thought shit was sweet and he didn't have to pay me because I was in confinement. That bitch nigga had another thing coming as soon as they let me out of the shit hole I was in. My boy, Cee, wanted to touch him but I told him to fall back, 'cause that ass was mine. See, everybody on the compound knew I didn't fuck off when it came to my bread. So, it was out of the ordinary for any nigga to think he could buck on my cash and pay me when he got ready. Nah, shit didn't work that way and now he knew that. From now on, it was on sight until I got that dough.

There was a light tap on the door. "Aye yo', Daman."

I recognized that voice from anywhere. "The window open, nigga. I ain't doing shit."

The door flap opened and the bright light from the hallway beamed inside the cell. Cee had a big, dumb-ass grin on his face. "Shit, ain't no tellin' what a nigga walkin' up on when it comes to you. I done caught you enough to last me until my bid up, nigga."

He wasn't lying, so I chuckled and got up from my bunk. "Big facts, nigga. You know how I get down. I'm nasty than a muthafucka."

"Don't I know it?" Cee's head swiveled from side to side as he checked his surroundings. "The compound going crazy and they been doing random shakedowns, so I didn't bring the phone out."

I leaned against the door. "Fuck going on out there?"

"These niggas been fighting and shit on the yard. They getting high as fuck and trippin', that's all."

"I done told them dumb muthafuckas to stop smoking them lizard tails at yard call."

Cee looked to the left, then back at me. "That ain't happening and you know that shit."

"Sooner or later there won't be a lizard in sight and they ass gone be shit out of luck." The topic of lizard tails wasn't on my agenda so I switched subjects quick. "Yo, this what I need you to do."

I stood straight up and walked to the window so we could be standing face to face. "Listen, I need you to get the phone out and hit up Rock. Find out if that nigga is laying on a cold slab."

"What nigga?" His forehead wrinkled out of curiosity.

Cee was my nigga, but my business was just that. Mine. The subject matter I was referring to was on a need-to-know basis and I didn't feel obligated to disclose any details. So, I shut that shit down quick.

"Just do what I told you to do and don't worry about who I'm talking about. Some shit needs to be left unsaid."

Cee looked at me and nodded his head with his mouth twisted. "Oh, so it's like that, huh?"

"This is outside business and I don't need nobody in it. Simple as that. So stop with all the twenty questions like you my bitch."

"That's cool, boss. No pressure."

He was mad as fuck, but I didn't care. "Good. Let me know if Zuri calls."

"A'ight."

As far as I was concerned our conversation was over, so I walked away. The sound of the window closing soon followed. I knew Cee felt some type of way with me being secretive, but I couldn't risk it. My time was getting shorter and I wasn't jeopardizing that with a new case. We were cool and all cause I used to fuck with his mama a while back, but that wasn't enough for me to utilize him as my personal diary. It was safer that way, because I would never tell on myself.

See, my boy had a murder charge that carried a fifteen-year bid. He was five years in, but he still had a long way to go. In my eyes, I wasn't trusting any man with a lengthy bid who could carry a bone back to a prosecutor for a reduced sentence. With my time winding down, I had to be careful with my actions. So, the quicker I got out, the better.

Zuri was in the free world making fucked-up decisions, while trying to live her best life. Guidance was what she needed and I was the only man that could steer her down the right path. Once I got out and we were face-to-face, I knew all of that shit she was talking was going to be out the window, because I was gone whip her ass back into shape. That Brick character fucked up my baby's train of thought and now, I had to go back and reprogram her way of thinking. Not to mention that bullshit ass job that was filling her head with all that righteous talk. Zuri's loyalty was a bit shaky, because she continued to let muthafuckas come between us. They wasn't doing shit, but polluting her brain and making her think something was wrong with our relationship.

"They all got me fucked up." I growled like an angry beast and punched the concrete wall hard as fuck.

"That's for you, Zuri." The skin on my knuckles split open to the white meat and blood streamed from my hand. That shit didn't faze me one bit. I raised my hand to my mouth and sucked the blood.

"I never thought I would have to put my hands on you, but you gone learn. Oh yeah, you gone learn."

I got down on the hard floor and started doing push-ups. As my body rose up and down, I continued to vent to myself. "I owe you for fucking that nigga while I was on the phone," I huffed in between sentences.

"For getting pregnant. And," I exhaled to catch my breath. "For talking to me sideways, like a nigga got a life sentence or some shit. You acting just like yo' mama."

The anger in me was boiling like hot grits and my speed increased tremendously. "I ain't gone kill her, but I'ma beat her ass one good time, for all the shit she took me through over the last several months." My arms felt tight, but I kept going. "Uh. Uh. Uh. Yes, I am."

***

Brick

It felt really good to have my baby girl back in my possession. The time she spent in the hospital was too long for me, but I thanked God for allowing her to pull through. Now, it was time for the healing process. The sound of her voice and laughter lit up the room and that was what I missed the most. She was definitely my pride and joy.

Breanna, Zuri and I sat on the floor having a tea party. That was what she enjoyed doing the most and I was willing to do anything to put a smile on her face. Even if that meant sippin' fake tea from a cup with my pinky finger up.

"Daddy, would you like a refill?" Breanna picked up her kettle and pretended to fill my cup.

"I guess I will." I chuckled, then raised the cup to my lips while taking a sip. "Woo, you make the best tea, baby."

"Yeah, I know." She was cheesing hard, as she poured her imaginary tea inside Zuri's cup.

"Ooh, this is good, Bre." Zuri sipped from her cup as well.

"This is my specialty." Bre sat her doll in her lap. "Ms. Kitty loves my tea too."

"I bet she do," I replied.

The sound of a ringing phone echoed through the room, silencing us for that moment. Assuming it was my phone, I reached into my pocket and pulled it out, but the screen was pitch-black. That was when I realized it was Zuri's phone. I watched her pick it up, look at the screen and sit it face down on the floor. Her actions didn't sit too well with me, so of course I called her out on my suspicions.

"Who is that?" My brow raised slightly.

Not once did Zuri look at me. It was like she was avoiding all eye contact. "Nobody."

The phone stopped, but it started back up again and that time, she made no effort to get it period. The last thing I wanted was to start an argument in front of my daughter, but she was testing a nigga's patience with that slick shit. "Sounds like nobody wants to speak to somebody real bad."

My words dripped in sarcasm and Zuri finally looked at me, but she tilted her head slightly in Breanna's direction. "Don't do that."

Once again the ringing stopped, but then a chime came through, signaling a notification. My stare was hard because she needed to see I was getting mad. "Nah, you stop, before I act a fool in here."

Bre's head swiveled back and forth between me and Zuri. "Are you two having a fight?"

The innocence in her eyes made me tone down for my princess. I didn't like for her to see me upset. "No, baby. Daddy's just playing with Zuri."

"Okay." Bre shook her finger at me. "You have to be nice to her."

"I will, baby."

Quickly standing on my feet, I walked over to Zuri and reached out for her. "Come on, let's talk." Even though she grabbed my hand so I could pull her up, I could feel the resistance. Once I had her on her feet, I looked down at Bre. "We'll be right back, okay?"

She was so into her doll, she didn't bother looking up. "Okay, Daddy," she whispered.

I escorted Zuri into the bedroom and closed the door behind us. It was time to get to the bottom of this damn mystery, before I lost my cool and blew a damn head gasket.

She sat down on the bed, so I stood in front of her with my arms folded across my chest. "So, you ready to tell me who keep blowing yo' shit up, or do I need to check for myself?"

Her shoulders tensed up out of fear. I knew she didn't like when I yelled at her, but at that moment, I didn't give a fuck. My only concern was who the fuck was she ignoring and why. She looked up at me and held her phone out. "It's Daman."

That nigga was lucky he was locked up, 'cause I would've paid his ass a visit a long time ago. "What the fuck do he want?"

Zuri shrugged her shoulders. "I don't know. When he called me while I was in California, I told him don't call me anymore. But, the text message says it's someone he locked up with, named Cee."

"Cee?" I scratched my head because I knew a Cee. "What's his real name?"

"I don't know. He brown-skinned, with a brush cut," she replied.

"And, how do you know that?" I asked.

"I saw him at visitation a few times and on video chat." Zuri placed both hands on her thighs and rubbed them repeatedly. I didn't know if it was from her nervousness or out of habit.

I opened the message and read it before I handed the phone back to her. "Call him back and put it on speaker."

Zuri did like I told her. The phone rang twice before someone picked up. "Hello."

"Aye, Zuri, this Cee. What's going on?" he shouted into the phone.

"Nothing," she snapped. "And, I hope you not calling to deliver a message for Daman, because I don't want to hear shit he has to say. I already told him to stop calling me."

"Nah, he ain't tell me to call you. I'm doing this on my own. He in the hole."

Zuri and I made eye contact. My first thought was to speak up, but something told me to be quiet and just listen. That voice sounded real familiar. "Well, I don't care where he's at and I hope that's not why you calling."

"Listen, I don't know how you gone take this, but hear me out and think before you respond."

"I'm listening." She rolled her eyes hard, clearly displaying no interest in what he was about to say.

"Okay, so I know your dude, Brick." My brow shifted because he confirmed what I knew already.

Zuri didn't hide the surprised look on her face. "How do you know him?"

"I know him from the hood. We used to get money together. Tell him it's Chauncey." He paused for a second. "And, that's why I'm telling you this, so make sure you relay the message to him."

"Okay. I will." Now he had her attention.

"Daman has a hit out on you and Brick. Well, he wants blood from Brick and only for you to lose the baby you carrying. I don't know what you did or said to him, but he ain't stopping until Brick is dead and you no longer pregnant."

"What?" Zuri shook her head from side to side. "No. Unh-unh. Daman wouldn't go that far."

"Do you hear yourself? This is Daman we talking about. And you know what he's capable of doing. Where is Brick anyway? I ain't talk to that nigga in a while."

"I'm right here, dirty. What's good?" I took the phone from Zuri and sat down beside her.

"Shit, bruh. Just maintaining in this bitch," Cee replied.

"So, back to this nigga having a hit on me. What that shit about?" All I wanted to know was if that was who shot at me. Daman had me fucked up if he thought I was gone let this shit slide and especially talking about getting rid of my seed.

"The nigga in lock-up, so he asked me to hit up his homie, Rock, and see if he had the body on a cold slab and shit. So, when I asked him who he was talking about, he wouldn't tell me. He was acting all secretive and shit. So, when I hit up Rock and told him Daman told me to call him, he filled me in on everything. That's how I found out it was you he was talking about."

When I looked to my left, Zuri was rocking back and forth, biting her nails. She had to bounce, because I didn't need her to hear the way the conversation was about to take a drastic turn. "Baby, go in the room with Bre and I'll be out in a minute."

"Okay." Surprisingly, she didn't fight with me. She got up and walked out the room. Probably because she couldn't fathom the idea of Daman putting her in harm's way, just because he was unhappy with her decision to move on and live a healthy, happy life with the king.

"A'ight. Quick question, is this nigga Rock a white dude?"

"Hell, yeah. He a big ass, lumberjack cracka. You can't miss that big ass muthafucka by a longshot."

"Yeah, that's who shot at me not too long ago." I couldn't believe the shit I was hearing, but I knew he wasn't lying. "Now it all makes sense."

"What's that?"

"I saw that muthafucka sitting across the street from Zuri's house one day when I was leaving. He put a tracker on my car and that's how he caught me off-guard."

"Damn, bruh. What you gone do?" Chauncey asked.

"I'm gone handle that nigga. Give me his number."

"A'ight. I'ma text it to her phone when we hang up."

"I got a job for you too."

"What's that?" Cee questioned.

"Take out Daman and I'll shoot you some cash for your troubles." I stroked my beard, as I awaited his reply.

"How much you talking?"

"I'll send you five bands."

"Five bands?" he repeated. "I was thinking more along the lines of ten bands."

I couldn't blame the nigga for trying, but that shit wasn't happening. He was gone take what I offered and step. "How much you think you gone get if Daman find out you told us about his plan? You think he gone let you live?" The line became silent and all I could hear was his heavy breathing. "I didn't think so."

"A'ight, bruh. I gotcha."

"A'ight. I'll send you seven for looking out."

"Bet. I'll hit you up when it's done."

"Yeah." After I hung up the phone, I took a deep breath to collect my thoughts. Once I was level-headed, I bopped towards the door and that was when the text came in with Rock's number.

I smiled because Daman and Rock better count their last fuckin' days.

Chapter 13

Deja

"I can't believe that selfish muthafucka took my child from the hospital without telling me or giving me the chance to see her." I pouted and flopped down on the sofa with my lip poked out.

"I don't know why," Erin sat down beside me. "You've been knowing him long enough to know he's not playing with you about Breanna."

"That doesn't matter, because he is wrong all day. He act like I can't see my own fuckin' daughter, with his nasty ass."

Erin tooted her nose in the air and shook her head like something was stinking. "You need to really stop. That don't make any sense how you acting."

Her reply was pissing me off because for one, she was supposed to be my best friend and two, why the fuck did she always feel the need to defend his ass? My inner ratchet came out the minute I started smacking my lips, talking with my hands and rolling my neck. "Like sus, help me out cause I'm confused."

"About what?" She in turn rolled her neck.

"Why you always taking his side? I'm supposed to be your best friend, but every time it comes to him, I see otherwise. I swear, I'm not feeling the love, period."

Erin sucked her teeth like I was getting on her nerves. "Deja, let's be real. You wrong all day. First you fucked his cousin, his first cousin at that and you have the audacity to call him nasty? Like have you ever sat back and thought about why he treats you the way he do?"

"Hmm." I grabbed my lips and nodded my head. "Okay, I see what it is now. You really on his side right now, but anyway, let's not forget that he fucked Dana."

"Girl, you and Dana weren't even friends, so you can't compare those situations, because they are totally different. What you did was foul as fuck, sis, and you know it."

My facial expression must've been worth a thousand words, as I examined her with piercing eyes. The shit she was saying was just over the top and unnecessary. She act just like Brick didn't cheat on me first. Shit, it wasn't my fault he went to prison and I ended up fucking Gucci.

Erin turned her body to face me. "And, before you say anything sideways, I wouldn't be a friend if I didn't tell you the truth. So, tread lightly when you question my friendship. And furthermore, this ain't even about you. It's about Breanna and her well-being."

"Nah, hold up." I put my hand up in front of her face. "So, what you trying to say? I can't take care of my own fuckin' child?"

Erin gave me the side eye. "You being reckless and aggressive right now, so move your hand." It wasn't intentional. I was just aggravated about the whole thing, so I allowed my hand to fall in my lap.

"Now, you know damn well what I meant. All I'm saying is just let him keep her. You can always see her and you know that. Brick loves Bre and she loves him. Their bond is so special and you know it. Besides, he's been gone five years, let the man catch up on the time he missed out on."

"Okay and who fault is it that he went to prison? Not mine." I said that with so much conviction.

"That didn't stop you from spending his money, did it? Nor did you tell him to stop. Y'all females a trip. It was all good when he was doing wrong to take care of you, but the minute he got jammed up, it was a problem. That's crazy."

Erin stood up and walked away, but she wasn't getting off that easily. "Well, just tell me how you really feel, because it's obvious you feel some type of way about this whole situation."

She stopped abruptly in her tracks, causing me to hit the brakes on my own feet. When Erin turned to face me, she had this evil look in her eyes. "Bitch, you really taking shit the wrong way, but that's just like you to take everything to the extreme."

My intention wasn't to make her that upset with me, but she acted like she wanted to hit me. Now, I didn't want to fight her, but if that's what we needed to do to get past this whole ordeal, then I was willing to boot up. Erin stood there breathing like a fire-breathing dragon ready to burn my ass, so I tried to make light of the situation and turn it into a laughing matter. "So, so, I don't care. You can get mad all you want to, but you know I love you, you love me, we're a happy family. With a great big hug and a kiss from me to you, won't you say you love me too?"

My Barney song didn't work because she was still frowning, but I was feeling hella childish. "Well, I guess you mad and since you are, you need to pick a side."

"I'm not picking shit. This is the thing that pisses me off." Erin let out a loud grunt and ran her hand across her face.

So, to make matters worse, I continued to push her buttons for the simple fact that she was butt-hurt over my actions. "Pick. A. Side." I clapped my hands after every word spoken.

"Brick and I have been sister and brother for years. We never fucked, kissed or nothing and we never felt that way about each other. We came up together from the dirt and I feel like it's my fault he going through all this bullshit. I was trying to set my brother up with someone I thought would treat him right, hold him down and bring out the best in him, but a bitch couldn't do that right. My brother a good-ass nigga, dawg, and you didn't deserve to be on his arm, period."

The words that fell from the person I thought was my friend stung badly and I couldn't believe it had come to that. In my eyes, that meant one thing. She been felt that way about me and it finally surfaced.

"Damn," I sighed. "That's how you really feel about me, huh? They said all you had to do was make a person mad and their true feelings would surface."

There was so much egg on my face and I wanted to cry, but I couldn't allow her to see me shed tears over her words. Instead, I walked around her and went to my front door and opened it. "You know, I really appreciate your honesty, but it's time for you to leave. I really thought you were a friend. Seems to me like you in love with Brick your damn self and if you really feel that way about him, then so be it. You are free to fuck and suck him if you like."

Erin turned around to face me. "It's funny you say that, because I've been more of a friend than you have been to me. It's all good though, ain't no love lost."

She stood at the threshold of my door and looked me dead in the eyes. "I'm not like you and I would never fuck up someone else's household. That's not my thing. Brick is finally happy and that gives me great joy to see him smile."

"Sure, he's happy. That's why he so fuckin' mad about me and Gucci. That gave me great joy to see the pain in his eyes." I rocked back and forth on my heels with a devious smirk on my face.

"Girl, he not mad because y'all fucked. He mad at the way y'all did that shit so casually in front of his daughter. He don't give a fuck about you."

"That's what you think." I replied.

"Nah, it's what I know. That man is about to marry Zuri and have another baby, so he's not thinking about your ass."

Those words hit me straight in the gut and I was damn near speechless. "Baby?"

"Yep. Breanna about to have a sister or a brother. They about to play house with your daughter, but hell it ain't like you really want her anyway." She was smiling hard, like she was trying to hurt me intentionally. "Don't sound hurt now. You wanted Gucci, remember?"

"Girl, fuck you." I tried to close the door, but she pushed it back open. "Bye."

"Oh, and you can forget about Gucci too because his girlfriend, Mehzani, which is Zuri's sister, got him on lock. So, it looks like you lost to a set of sisters."

Erin walked off and I just stood there stuck at everything she had just revealed to me. It was bad enough he had another baby on the way, but to hear them hoes was sisters bothered me the most. I finally found the strength to close the door. All I wanted was to crawl up in my bed and cry myself to sleep, but first I needed to shake shit up a bit. I was tired of being used and abused.

***

Brick

Ever since Cee hit me with that Daman bullshit, I been on savage mode. That shit had me ready to go ape shit around that bitch. To put a hit out on me was one thing, but to involve my future wife and child was below the belt. Not to mention off limits and suicide in his case. It was crazy that he was willing to put Zuri's life on the line, his own flesh and blood. But, I guess that didn't make a difference, since he didn't have a problem fucking her. That blood shit went straight out the window, along with his morals and values. Daman was a cold-hearted, evil muthafucka, but he finally met his match when he came for me and mine. He put his own nail in the coffin and all I was waiting on was that phone call to let me know it had been handled.

Before I left the house, I told Zuri I was going out to handle business, but before I did anything I scooped my ace up first. Coop was in disbelief that Daman could be so cruel.

"So, you mean to tell me this nigga put a hit out on you and his daughter because he don't want y'all together?"

I nodded my head, as I parked the car. "Yeah, man. The nigga is a fucked-up individual."

See, I never told Coop about the history between Zuri and Daman. We were close, but that was one thing I couldn't disclose about my girl. I knew what she went through constantly and I didn't want to paint that type of picture in his head about her. Also, it was my job to protect her peace and privacy, so I kept that to myself. No one needed to know what she went through, except for me.

"Damn. I know sis going through it right now," he replied with empathy.

"Yeah, but I got my baby. I would never let anything happen to her, which is why I told Cee to handle that nigga and I'd send him seven racks for his trouble."

"Now all we gotta do is find this hillbilly ass nigga and do his ass in."

"Facts."

When I killed the engine in the car, that was our cue to get out and be on our way. As we walked towards the building I looked over at my dawg. "This nigga is a party animal, but he solid. You'll pick up on his vibe as soon as you meet him."

"You know I stay on alert."

The bouncer wasn't standing at the door when we walked up, but as soon as we got on the inside he was standing at attention.

"What up, Brick?" He dapped me up, but his eyes were on Coop.

"Coolin'. This my homie, Coop. You'll be seeing him more often when I come through.

"I'll keep that in mind." He turned to Coop and dapped him up as well. "What's up, homie?"

"Shit. Just catching the vibe." Coop was checking out the waitress that walked pass us with the fat ass.

"It's a good vibe in here. I'm sure you'll love it." The bouncer grinned and turned his attention back to me. "Hector in the back."

"A'ight, bet that up." I hit Coop on the arm. "This way."

To my surprise, Hector wasn't in the booth when we made it to the back, but he was definitely on it. There was an open bottle of Louis XIII sitting in an ice bucket.

"This nigga gettin' lit." Coop laughed and sat down.

"Already." Just as I was about to fix myself a glass, the same waitress Coop was checking out stepped in, smiling.

"The boss will be out in just a moment, but he said for you and your friend to help yourselves to anything." The way she emphasized on the *anything* part, told me she was on that menu as well.

Coop ate that shit right on up. "Anything, huh?" he licked his lips and stroked the hair on his chin.

The Spanish shorty ran her hand across her ass and down her thigh to her garter and pulled it. "Anything." I guess she was feeling him too. She had to be about five-five, weighing a buck thirty-five with long, jet black hair.

"You a fool, man." I grabbed the bottle and poured myself a shot.

"You want one, bruh?"

"Hell, yeah. I ain't about to be the only sober one in this bitch while y'all turn up." He reached for an empty glass from the table, but she stopped him.

"Let me get that for you." She leaned forward and one of her titties popped out, exposing her light brown nipple.

"Damn." Coop looked at me and grinned. "So, you been holding out all this time on me, huh? No wonder it always take you long to leave from here."

"Nah. You know it ain't like that. My queen at home, so I come in and handle business, then I'm out."

"I hear ya." He didn't sound too convinced, but he knew me better than that.

"Here you go." She walked up to him and sat the glass on his lap, but she didn't let it go until he grabbed it.

Coop looked down at his lap and then back up at her. "I see you curious."

"Maybe," she winked. "You want a lap dance?"

"And your phone number." He took a sip of the Yak.

"Okay."

Two Chainz's, "I Luv Dem Strippers" was playing, so she turned her back towards him and put her ass in his face. That nigga was cheesing hard as fuck while he watched her dance. I just sat back and watched my nigga enjoy himself. He was a bachelor now, so I knew he was about to be sticking and moving.

When the song was over shorty stopped dancing and turned back to face him.

"You can get my number on your way out. I have to get back to work, enjoy."

"Bet that up." Coop watched her and that fat ass walk away.

"Boy, you wild," I laughed.

"I'm free, bruh, so I'm just vibing. It ain't like I'm trying to wife the bitch up. I just wanna fuck and get my dick sucked. That's it." Coop downed his drink and sat the glass down on the table.

"Be safe, my nigga. That's all I can tell you." A shadow at the entrance caught my attention, so I looked over in that direction and realized it was Hector.

He waltzed his happy ass in there with two females at his side and a cigar in his hand. It looked like he had just finished fucking, since he was so relaxed in his black and gold robe and slippers.

"Brick!" he shouted with his arms extended. "My man." Hector walked in and shook my hand. "How's it going?"

"Shit will be better once we handle this little situation." I took the entire shot to the head and sat the glass down as well.

"This your number-two?" he asked.

"Yeah," I replied before introducing them. "Hector, this Coop. My right-hand man and best friend."

Hector reached out to Coop and they shook hands. "Nice to meet you, new friend. I hope you enjoyed my gracious hospitality."

"I did. Thank you."

"Any friend of Brick's is a friend of mine." Hector adjusted his robe and took a seat. The women he came in with were still standing. He snapped his fingers. "The two of you are dismissed."

Both chicks turned on their heels and left the booth. Coop was impressed and I could tell by the look on his face.

"You got they asses trained," he chuckled. "That's what I'm talm 'bout."

"That's how it should be. Stick around and I'll teach you a little something." Hector crossed his legs and puffed on his cigar. "So, what's the latest news?" He didn't waste any time getting straight to the purpose of the meeting.

"I need a trace on a phone number. It's for the nigga that shot at me and put the tracker on my car," I explained.

"Okay. I can have someone look into that for me and I'll let you know what we find." Hector paused and scratched his temple. "Now, it's my turn to ask you for a favor."

"Whatever you need me to do." Somehow I knew I would have to return the favor one day.

"It may get a little bloody, but I know you don't have a problem with getting your hands dirty."

"Nah. You already know that's my background and getting dirty is what I do."

Coop nodded his head in agreeance. "Straight like that."

"My nigga." I dapped him up and looked over at Hector. "And, I got my number-two, who down for the cause."

Whatever job he had for me, I was ready for it. He had my back and it was only right that I had his in return. Coop's participation wasn't a question or a doubt, because I already knew he was gone ride with me on any mission handed down.

Chapter 14

Zuri

"Oh my God!" I screeched with my mouth agape and hand over it. I was so excited that I couldn't contain my emotions. We spent the past few days, searching high and low for a property, and we finally found the perfect spot to set up shop.

"This is the one right here." The building I was viewing was everything, so as we did the walk-through, I took some pictures.

"You like it?" the realtor asked, while walking slowly behind me as I admired every square foot on the marble tile.

"Like it.?" I spent around in a full circle with my arms out. "I love it." Breanna was limping behind me slowly, being that she still had the cast on her leg. I kneeled down and fixed the barrette on her ponytail. "Do you like it, Bre?"

"It's pretty."

"Good. Your daddy is going to be very happy." I stood up to face the realtor. "Let's move forward with the paperwork."

"Okay. Let's do it. I have everything you need in the car." I grabbed Breanna's hand and we exited the building en route to the realtor's car.

Brick was going to want every single detail, so I made sure to gather all the information. "So, Jeff, how long do you think it would take to get everything done?"

"It shouldn't take no longer than a week. You have the full deposit on hand right?"

"Yes." He closed the passenger door. "If you like, you can come down to my office and complete the application."

I thought about it for a second, but realized that Bre didn't need to be out much longer. It was time to elevate her leg. "No. I need to get my daughter in the house so she can rest and I will drop it off tomorrow morning."

Jeff licked his lips and handed me the packet. "I'll be waiting." The way he held my hand captive didn't sit too well with me, so I pulled away from him.

"I'll see you tomorrow at the office."

"Have a good day, beautiful."

The last thing I needed was for Breanna to tell her daddy anything that man said, so I ended that conversation quick. I knew without a doubt that Brick would have a fit if he caught wind of any of this. I grabbed Bre by the arm and headed to my car that was parked only a few feet away.

"Zuri, I'm hungry." Breanna's voice was so sweet and innocent, it made me smile.

"Okay, baby. What would you like?"

"McDonald's."

"Hmm." I lifted her up so she could climb into the back seat. "How about some Chick-Fil-A? Me and the baby don't like McDonald's."

"Okay."

Once she was in her seat, I fastened the seatbelt and closed the door before going to the other side. When I got into the car, I decided to call Brick to let him know the good news. The phone rang several times before he picked up.

"What's up, baby?"

"Hey, my love. I have good news." My cheekbones were high as hell, as I grinned from ear to ear.

"Oh, yeah? What's that?"

"I found a place and it's beautiful."

"Oh, yeah? I wanna see it."

"I took some pictures of it, so I can show you when you get home." I pulled out onto the road, en route to our destination. The three of us were hungry and couldn't wait much longer.

The Chick-Fil-A drive-thru was crowded as hell and I refused to sit in that long ass line. Although I didn't want to drag Bre out the car again, I had to because I could no longer hold my pee. When I parked the car and looked back at her, she frowned.

"We have to get out again?"

"Yes, baby. I'm sorry."

"But my legs hurt," she whined.

"This is the last stop before we go home," I promised.

Breanna didn't respond. Instead, she waited patiently until I made it to the passenger side and helped her out the backseat.

"Woo! Girl, you heavy." I joked, while lifting her from the car and placing her feet first on the ground.

"My daddy said you heavy too." Her sassiness was so cute to me. I couldn't wait until I found out what I was having at my appointment in a few days. Since I could remember, I always wanted my first child to be a boy, so he could protect his sister. But, now that I was more hands-on with Breanna, I wanted to have my own mini-me. In the end, as long as the baby was healthy, that was all that really mattered to me.

"He did, huh? Well, it's his fault I'm heavy anyway."

"Why?" Bre touched my stomach. "Did he put the baby in here?"

Her comment almost made me choke on my spit because I wasn't sure how I should respond. Apparently I said too much and now she wanted additional answers. While I thought of a good response, I grabbed her hand and ushered her across the parking lot.

"I guess you can say that."

"How did he put the baby in there?" She continued to probe with her nosey ass. That girl been on the planet six years and had questions like she was an adolescent.

"We prayed for it. Now, come on, so we can get our food."

"Well, when I get older, I'm gonna pray for a baby too," she replied.

"I don't think your dad is going to like that very much."

After our little trip to the ladies room, we ordered our food and waited on my name to be called. The inside wasn't as packed as the outside was, so that was a blessing in itself. While we waited, a familiar face entered the establishment and stood in line. I watched from afar, because it had been a while since I'd spoken to him, and that was due to Brick and his demands. It was like he could feel my presence. His head swiveled in my direction and a huge smile spread across his lips, as he walked towards me.

"Hey, Zuri." Jason walked up and gave me a hug. At first, I was hesitant, but I hugged him back.

"Hey, Jason. How are you?"

"I'm good. You know we miss you at work?" He sat down in the booth next to Bre. "Hey, cutie." She looked at him with a mean mug. That girl was certainly Brick's child.

Jason laughed. "Oh, she ain't friendly at all."

"No, she's not."

"What's your name?" he asked her.

Bre looked at him for a while before she responded, "Michelle Obama."

Jason and I burst out into laughter. "I like that," he replied. Then, he reached in his pocket and pulled out his wallet.

"That's Breanna, Brick's daughter."

"Oh," he cleared his throat. "Well, that explains a lot."

I ignored his comment and changed the subject. "So, y'all miss me at work?"

"Of course. How is the pregnancy going? Everything good?" Jason pulled out two dollars and handed it to Bre. "Tell Zuri to take you to get ice cream."

"Thank you." Bre took the money and put it inside her pocket.

"You're very welcome." Jason turned back to me. "I've been trying to call you, but you know that already."

All I could do was shake my head. "You know why you haven't been able to talk to me. I'm not trying to mess up what I have going on. Nothing good can from that, besides a rift."

"So, you would really let him ruin our friendship just like that? Come on Zuri, I've known you longer."

"I wouldn't allow it." I paused to look at Bre, then handed her my phone. Hopefully, "Baby Shark" would keep her occupied until we left. "It would be different if I didn't know how you really felt and because of that, I have to keep my distance from you."

His brow creased. "You want me to apologize for that?"

"No. I just want you to respect my feelings and relationship." I kept my voice as low as possible. "There has to be boundaries and I don't feel like you would comply."

"Damn, Z. I'm crushed." There was sadness in his eyes, but I couldn't do anything about that. "I love you so much and—"

Before he could finish I cut him off. "Stop right there."

In the nick of time, they called my name, so I got up immediately. "Come on, Bre. Our food is ready."

Jason got up, so she could get out the booth with his assistance. I grabbed her hand and rushed to the counter. It was time for us to go before he said anything else out the way. He was a good friend, but he knew for a fact there couldn't be more than that. With every attempt made to escape him, Jason was hot on my trail in the parking lot.

"I'm sorry, Zuri. Just slow down for a minute."

"Jason, I have to go. Come on, Bre, climb in."

I attempted to help her, but Jason managed to wedge himself in between the both of us so he could help her. While he fastened her in, I went to the driver's side and got in the car. The minute he closed the door would be the minute I pulled off. As soon as the door closed, that was exactly what I did. Jason was calling my name, but I ignored him and kept it moving. We weren't down the street good before he was calling my phone. I was going to ignore it, but since we were no longer face-to-face, I was good with that.

"Yeah."

"Why you pulled off on me like that? That's crazy," Jason sighed. "You treat me like some random nigga off the streets."

"Can you understand where I'm coming from? I don't need the added stress and talking to you doesn't make it any better. That's the main reason we don't talk now. If you would just be a friend, then we would be okay. But no, you steady pushing the envelope to a house that's no longer vacant. I'm taken and having a baby. That should be enough to make you fall back and just be my friend."

"I know and I'm sorry. Every time I tell myself that when I get the chance to talk to you, I would keep it on a friendly basis, but that's hard to do when you love someone."

"Jason, stop saying that." My emotions were surfacing and I didn't like it one bit. "Please," I whispered.

"I will. Have a nice life, Zuri. I wish you nothing but the best of luck." Jason hung up the phone without warning, so I sat it down in my lap.

Jason's actions had me so confused because I never led him on or made him think that we would be a couple. So, I didn't understand how he still felt the same way, after so much time had passed. It didn't matter what he said or did, Brick was the man I wanted and I wasn't about to let him go or ruin a good thing. My man was a Godsend and he gave me my biggest blessing. Not only that, but he came into my life when it was dark and helped me out of a situation I didn't think was possible to get out of. My phone vibrated and chimed at the same time signaling a text message. When I opened it, all I could do was shake my head.

Scam Likely: Zuri, I am truly sorry and I hope this doesn't affect our friendship. I just want you to understand where I'm coming from. I love you and I always pictured you and me together. That baby you're carrying is supposed to be mine. No other man, but you NEVER gave me a chance to get that far with you. You broke my heart when you showed up to work flaunting that baby bump like you were so happy. When your nigga fucked up, I just knew I had a chance, but you took him back and that shit crushed my soul. It's cool though, because this will be my last text to you. I really do wish you the best. I'll always love you.

Jason had me so hot that I threw my phone on the floor of the passenger side. The man was really fucking with me when he knew damn well there wasn't going to be nothing between us. That was the main reason I didn't communicate with him. It didn't matter that I put him in the friend zone, since his ass was always trying to trespass. He was definitely a good catch, but just not for me and that was what he couldn't accept. If I would've disclosed my deepest and darkest secrets to him, he wouldn't be able to stand in the paint. That was factual, because Brick is a hood nigga and he had a hard time accepting it, but his love for me outweighed all of that.

After traveling for what seemed like forever, we finally made it home and I was ready to go inside and kill my food. I knew Breanna was ready to do the same.

"We're home, baby." I looked back to see what she was doing.

"About time, 'cause I'm starving."

All I could was laugh. "Me too."

As I stepped from the car, I noticed a police car posted in the parking lot. "Hmm. I wonder what the hell happened over here for him to be trolling."

It was unusual to see the police present in the neighborhood Brick lived in, but I guess that was a good thing. That wasn't my business, so I got Bre from the back seat and gathered up my belongings and walked towards the building. My hands were completely full, so when I adjusted all the shit I was holding and passed Bre the food bag, I could hear footsteps behind me. When I looked up, there were two well-dressed men with badges on their hip.

"I'll get that for you, ma'am." One of them held the door open and smiled. "Hey cutie, is your name Breanna Riccardo?"

That shit blew me, so I paused and turned to face him. "Excuse me, but how do you know her name?"

"Are you Zuri Monroe?"

"Yes, I am. Now, what do you want?"

"I'm Detective Rogers and this is my partner, Detective Davidson. We need to talk to you about an important matter." He looked to the right and pointed towards the elevator. Then back at me.

"I don't even know what this about." I was annoyed by the whole ordeal and if this had something to do with Brick, I had nothing to say about my man.

"It's about Brandon Riccardo and I'll explain everything to you once we're inside."

My heart was racing like I had just drunk an energy drink. All I knew was, Brick better not be in no shit. I couldn't fathom having to raise my child alone if he had to go back to prison.

Chapter 15

Brick

Coop and I were slouched down in the seat doing a stakeout in the late afternoon. The sun hadn't gone down as of yet, but the office was off in a dead end by a lake, so we were good.

"As soon as they finish loading the truck, we gone bum rush that shit, lay them niggas down and take the whole truck."

My ace pulled the hammer back on his piece, sat it on his lap and slipped on a pair of black leather gloves. "I'm ready."

There were only two people at the transporting location and I couldn't understand that if they were delivering weight, why not have more shooters with them. Clearly, they weren't worried about being ambushed. We lied in wait for ten more minutes before they closed the back of the truck.

"Let's go," I instructed.

Coop and I slid from the front seat of the vehicle and crept across the street. While he targeted the passenger, I was focused on the driver. Together we ambushed both men.

"Put your fuckin' hands where I can see them and open the back of this truck."

The driver was startled by my presence, but he followed my command. Coop pushed the passenger to the back of the truck. "Get'cho ass back there."

"What do you want, money?"

"Did I say I wanted money? Now, shut up and open it." Once he unlatched the lock, he raised the door. Right away, I observed boxes of seafood. "Go up there and open one of those boxes so I can see what's in it."

"If you try anything I will blast your homie's brain all over the asphalt. Now, do it slowly." Coop pressed the steel to the back of his victim's head.

"Okay. Okay." The driver walked slowly with his hands up, until he stopped at the first box and opened it. He reached down inside the box and pulled out the cocaine.

"Put it back in the box and come on." I waved my gun in his direction.

"Who sent you?" he asked, as he walked towards me with his arms still in the air.

"Hector. You owe him money and you passed the deadline, so now it's time to pay the piper."

"Please, don't kill us," he pleaded. "We can give him back the work we lost."

"Y'all stole that shit," Coop added.

"Nah, it don't work that way. Who did you get this work from? It ain't come from Hector, so that means you went behind his back and found another connect."

"Javier," he replied and stood in front of me.

"Any last words or prayers, before I send you on your way?" I looked over at Coop's victim. "You too."

They both got down on their knees and spoke in Spanish. "Padre nuestro, que estás en el cielo. Santificado sea tu nombre. Venga tu reino. Hágase tu voluntad en la tierra como en el cielo. Danos hoy nuestro pan de cada día. Perdona nuestras ofensas, como también nosotros perdonamos a los que nos ofenden. No nos dejes caer en tentación y líbranos del mal. Amén."

As soon as they stopped, I nodded at Coop and we both pulled the trigger, firing one shot to the middle of their foreheads.

Pew! Pew!

Coop turned and looked at me. "Yo, what the fuck were they saying?"

"The Lord's Prayer. I guess they figured praying before execution would send them to heaven, but I highly doubt that."

My father was Cuban, so I spoke Spanish fluently, but that was something I never disclosed when doing business. No one would ever suspect it, because of my brown skin. To them, I was just another nigga from the hood and I was fine with those assumptions. That was my way of having one up on whoever I was dealing with. Hector has had plenty of conversations around me, thinking I didn't understand and that was the way I wanted to keep it. The day he ever tried to cross me, or say anything besides good shit about me, I was gone do his ass in and I put that on my mama.

"Let's clear it, bruh. Hop in the truck and I'll follow you."

"A'ight." Coop walked towards the truck and opened the door. "I'm not driving this bitch all over town either. One destination and that's it. Ain't no telling who gone be looking for this damn truck." He hopped into the driver seat and closed the door.

"We going to the warehouse he told us about and that's it. His men will handle it from there." I stood at the window. "Crank this bitch up, wat'chu waiting on?"

Coop looked me in the eyes and shook his head. "The keys not in the ignition."

"Shit," I huffed. "Let me check his pockets right quick." I jogged to the body and checked the driver's pockets and was in luck when I pulled out a set of keys.

"Aye, Brick, we got company," he yelled, just loud enough for me to hear.

"Fuck. How many?"

"The tint's too dark and I can't see."

"Stay low until we can see. Just be ready to shoot." The car pulled up slowly and stopped slightly in front of the truck.

No one got out the car. Then, I heard a phone start ringing beside me. It belonged to one of the dead men. After they called it twice, the passenger door opened and a big dude with a ponytail got out, wearing all-black. He looked at the truck and threw up a hand signal. Just like that, two other dudes got out the car wielding weapons, but I was ready to blast they ass as soon as they were close to the truck.

All three men walked slowly in a single-file line, as they approached the truck. With my finger on the trigger, I aimed in their direction and squeezed slowly. Before I could get a round off, I heard a shot.

Pew!

The dude with the ponytail hit the ground and I knew Coop had done set it off. I fired several shots in their direction and managed to take down one. The last one tried to run back to the car, but I chased him and put a bullet in his head.

"Go get in the car," Coop shouted.

"This car in the way," I replied.

"Fuck that car. I'm running through that shit."

Coop hit the gas and ran into the front of the car, crushing the frame until he was able to push it out the way. By that time, I was in my car pulling off and we were in the wind.

On the way to the warehouse, I got a phone call. I was hoping it wasn't Zuri, because when I was in my zone, I couldn't talk to her. It was something about doing wrong and worrying about my family that got to me. My phone was in the armrest, so when I finally pulled it out, I was relieved it was Hector.

"Hello."

"Did it go smooth?" he asked.

"I'm headed to you now."

"Good. I have a surprise for you when you get here."

"Cool." I hung up the phone and tossed it on the seat next to me.

On the way to the warehouse, my guards were up and on high alert. Everyone was a suspect. There was no telling who was watching and waiting on us to slip, so they could ambush us in return. Coop had to be doing at least fifty mph through the city, because we arrived in twenty minutes tops. We stuck to the main roads, just in case we were spotted. The chances of a shootout in the middle of traffic weren't likely at all. There was too much money at stake here.

Two bodyguards were standing at the gate when we pulled up. Both of them opened it up and stepped to the side, so we could gain entry. Once inside, we had to be let into the warehouse by another guard. That led us straight into the secluded building. Hector had his operation on lock and I knew I was gone have to step my game up. Secluded meeting spots was definitely on my to-do list.

146

We parked both vehicles and got out. Hector had a slight grin on his face as he approached us, dressed to the nines in an Armani suit. His favorite cigar was hanging from his lip, but he moved it once he was close to us.

"You know, I didn't know what to expect when I sent you over there, but I have to admit you surprised me. That, my friend, let me know I can depend on you."

"I told you I could do any job you placed in front of me."

Hector glanced at Coop. "New friend, you good in my book."

"That's what's up." He nodded his head.

"Now, for the surprise." Hector turned on his heels and started to walk off. "Follow me."

One of his henchmen shook his head and frowned as if he was disappointed. "No creo que tuvieras marido de su hermana muerto. Ella nunca va a perdonarte por eso."

Coop and I stopped in place to watch the bomb explode. He leaned in closer to me and whispered, "What the hell did he just say?"

I whispered back to him. "He said he can't believe he had his sister's husband killed and she will never forgive him for that."

Hector froze in place and swiveled his head in his flunky's direction. "Nunca me perdonar ¿Eh? ¿Y cómo coño hacer crees que ella va a saber? Sé que no lo que iba a confesar."

Before Coop could ask what was said, I beat him to the punch. "Hector just asked him how the fuck she gone find out and he ain't confessing to shit. This nigga a snitch."

"Snake-ass nigga. It's always the ones closest to you," Coop added.

"I. I don't know," the flunky stuttered, now realizing he was knee-deep in shit.

"You don't know, huh?" Hector nodded his head up and down, while easing his hand behind his back. All that point, all that was seen was a piece of steel raise in the air.

Boca!

He let off a single round into his flunky's forehead. Brain matter and blood spurt from the back of his head, as his body dropped to the floor.

Coop and I stood in place and waited on Hector to turn around and address the shit that just transpired before us. "That's what I do to snitches. He been with me for fifteen years, so he knew better."

"Well, he got what he deserved."

Hector nodded his head. "Come on." Then, he stepped over the body. Coop and I followed suit.

The walk was a short distance and we stopped in front of a closed door. Hector put his hand on the knob and opened it. "This is what's awaiting behind door number one for you."

When we stepped inside, there was a white male, hanging in the air by a thick ass chain. It was Rock. "Oh, yeah. I like this surprise." I smiled and rubbed my hands together.

"I knew you would." Hector stood off to the side while I approached Rock. His mouth was bleeding. From the looks of things, he had already gotten his ass beat.

I walked up on Rock and hit him dead in his face, while he looked me in the eyes. That nigga's head snapped back, but he didn't make a sound as the blood dripped from his bottom lip. He knew his fate and there was nothing he could do about it. The moment he decided to pull up on me and take shots, killed every piece of control he had upon his life. That decision was now in my hands. A slight tap on my shoulder got my attention. When I turned around, Hector was standing on the side of me.

"Torture away." He passed me a stun gun.

A wide grin spread across my lips. "Nah. I need something a little more painful than that." I looked around the warehouse and walked towards the counter where the tools were located. The nail gun caught my attention, so I picked it up. "Oh, yeah. This what the fuck I'm talm 'bout."

Casually, I walked towards Rock and stopped in front of him. "We gone cut straight to the chase. Who the fuck sent you?"

Even though I knew the answer, I wanted to hear it from his mouth. "You gone kill me either way, so I ain't saying shit."

"Oh, you tough, huh?" I turned on the power tool and waved it in his face. "Well, let's see how much a pig can take before it squeals."

The sound of the drill filled my ears as I squeezed the trigger, while pressing against his thigh. The tip broke through the skin and blood oozed from the open wound. Rock screamed loud and wiggled in place. "Ahh, shit!"

Instead of using the reversal button, I yanked the pointy shank from his thigh, causing him to yelp out in pain. "You ready to talk?" I asked, prepared to stick him again.

"Fuck you. I'm not saying shit."

"Wrong answer." After opting for a new hole, I drilled into his knee cap, tearing through flesh and bone. That time I used more force by pushing it deeper and holding the button down at the same time.

"Ahhh! You muthafucka." Rock squeezed his eyes tight and bit down on his lip, as if that would help the pain subside. His body trembled hard, like he was going into shock.

"You goddamn right. Speak up or look like Swiss cheese by the time this shit over." When he didn't reply, I took the initiative to make the pain worse by drilling hole after hole into all of his joints. The sound of bones cracking and painful screams filled the warehouse.

"Okay, okay. I give up." His breathing was intense and heavy.

My chuckle was loud, yet evil. The sound of mercy had finally presented itself, so I leaned closer to him and stopped the noise coming from the drill. "What was that? I couldn't hear you." Constant vibrating sensations tickled my thigh, but I ignored every call that came through. Whoever it was had to wait.

Rock sighed, releasing a loud grunt before replying. "It was Da.Da. Daman. He put the hit out on you."

"Why?"

"You took," his breathing had become shallow as he was fading in and out of consciousness, "his daughter away."

The reason angered me and thoughts of him violating Zuri flashed in my mind. I could hear her moans in my ear and I felt disgusted by it all. With the power drill in my hand, I raised it and smacked Rock over the head with it. The blood splatter was now airborne, but that didn't stop me. Repeatedly, I bashed his skull with the heavy tool, until I felt someone grab my arm.

"Bruh, stop. The nigga dead."

Coop took the drill from my hand and I didn't fight it. Rock's face was disfigured and his family was going to need dental records to identify him. I made sure of that. Blue and black bruises covered his skin, along with the bright red blood. After staring at him for a while, I walked off to get my thoughts together and check to see who was calling me. When I opened up the phone, I saw I had several missed calls and a text message.

Wifey: Please come home now! The police is here for Bre.

My heart skipped a beat and a million thoughts ran through my head as I dialed Zuri's number. There was only one person that could be behind some shit like that and it was Deja. The police had no reason to be at my house. The proper paperwork had been recently filed and my name is on her birth certificate. Zuri's phone went to voicemail and something came over me I hadn't felt since the day I got that call about Bre. And that was fear.

As I turned on my heels, prepared to fill Coop in on what was going down, he was already heading in my direction. Sweat beads were forming on my forehead, so I wiped them away.

"Bruh, we gotta bounce. Zuri texted me, talm 'bout the police at my place for Bre and now, she not answering the phone. Shit don't sound right."

"Shit, let's be out. Tell Hector we got an emergency."

"Yeah, a'ight." My baby came before anything, so I opted to call him on my way home to give him an update. Right now, I had to make sure they were safe. Fuck the rest.

Chapter 16

Zuri

"What's going on here? Nobody is telling me nothing and I'm getting aggravated." Breanna was in her room, while I sat in the living room, trying to figure out what the fuck was going on.

"We already told you that we waiting on Brick," Detective Rogers replied.

"Well, he not answering his phone as you can see, so y'all need to leave and come back when he here."

Detective Davidson stood up and adjusted his jacket. "I'm going to step outside for a moment. Be right back."

"Okay." He replied.

After hearing the door close, I glanced in that direction to see he had locked the door. To me, that meant he had no intention on coming back. Panic threatened my body, but I knew I had to remain calm for the sake of my child and Bre. Instead of questioning him, I remained seated, with a million thoughts running through my mind. There was something completely wrong with the entire scenario and I no longer felt comfortable. My only wish was that Brick would come busting in at any moment and get these fools out of here.

Detective Rogers looked in my direction with hunger in his eyes, as if he had found his prey. When he licked his lips, it made me cringe. That alone made me feel like I was in danger and I had to protect myself from this predator. Slowly scooting to the edge of the seat, I took a deep breath to display the struggle. The slimeball cop stood up and extended his hand.

"I'll help you up," he chuckled. "Looks like you having a hard time."

"I got it." Against my wishes, he grabbed my wrist and helped me up anyway.

"Where are you going?" he asked.

"To the bathroom. Why?" My reply was a little fly because I hated to be questioned, and especially by a man I wasn't fucking, period.

"Just asking."

"Oh okay, because you seem a little nosey." My plaits swung side to side as I walked down the hallway and into the bathroom. Just as I was closing the door, I saw a hand appear.

"What are you doing?" I shouted.

"Leave the door open, so I can see that pussy," Detective Rogers demanded in an angry tone while pushing the door towards me.

Forcefully, I pushed it back, because there was no way he was getting in without a fight. "No. Get the fuck out of here."

The fear in my heart gave me strength from somewhere, because I managed to get the door closed. I prayed that Breanna still had her headphones in while watching a movie. With all the commotion unraveling, I was certain it would bring her out the room. There was banging on the door.

"Let me in. I promise to be gentle."

I ignored his dumb-ass remark and dialed Brick's number. By the grace of God, he answered. "What's up, baby?"

"Brick, I'm scared, where are you?"

"Like ten minutes from the house. What's going on?"

"The detectives I told you about? I think they're a fraud. One of them is trying to get in the bathroom with me."

"Where is Bre?" His voice had become high-pitched.

"She's in the room. I told her don't come out until I come get her."

Boom! Boom!

"Open this fuckin' door before I kick it in."

"Baby, hurry up. I'm scared."

"Listen to me, open the cabinet underneath the sink and get the gun that's attached to the ceiling. When that muthafucka kick in that door, you blow his fuckin' brains out."

My hand trembled as I opened the door and felt around for the gun. The piece of steel grazed my fingertips. In a hurry, I unsnapped the holster and pulled it out.

"I got it."

"Do like I told you. Aim that muthafucka at the door and when he comes in, you let loose. Put the phone down, but leave it on speaker."

"Okay."

Tears were streaming down my face, but I didn't bother to wipe them. I sat the phone down on the sink and did like I was told. My eyes were trained on the door, as I watched the door cave in slowly, but surely.

"Baby, I'm scared," my voice trembled.

"I know, baby, but this ain't the time to be scared. You have to protect yourself and the kids, so shake it off."

His voice kept me sane, but I needed him there to protect me. That was his job as a man. However, I also knew he was right about it being my duty to protect me and mine in his absence. Time was winding down and I knew it would only be a matter of time before the aggressive pervert got in. As I wiped my face with my shirt, I took a deep breath and gave myself a pep talk, while sitting on the side of the tub.

"Family over everything, Zuri. You can do this." My heart was beating so damn hard, I thought I would have a heart attack in a matter of seconds. "Kill this bitch. Kill this bitch."

No sooner than I said that, the bathroom door came crashing in, slamming against the wall and Detective Rogers stepped in with a slight grin on his face. "Now, I have to be rough wit'…"

His eyes grew wide when he saw the barrel of the gun and we locked eyes. "Put the gun down."

Both of us were frozen in time.

"Zuri, pull the trigger," Brick screamed through the phone, but I remained silent with my finger on the trigger. "Zuri, pull the fuckin' trigger."

The irritation in his voice pulled me from my daze, but I still hesitated. I never shot one single person a day in my life, so it was hard to do it so easily. But at the same time, I knew my life was on the line, along with my kids'. The detective took one step towards me, while reaching behind his back. My finger hugged the trigger tightly, releasing a single round into his shoulder.

Boca!

His body jerked, but when that didn't stop him, I pulled the trigger once more. That time, the bullet hit him in the chest and bright red blood soaked through his dress shirt. Rogers dropped to his knees, then fell forward, hitting his head on the toilet on the way down.

"Zuri," Brick called my name, but I didn't answer because I was too busy making sure the bastard was dead.

My movements were swift, as I got up from the tub and moved towards the body. While I hovered over him, a crooked smile appeared and I felt damn good about what I had just done.

"Zuri, baby, I'm here. Are you okay?"

"Yeah, baby, he's dead." My eyes were trained on him to see if he was going to make a sudden move. From the looks of things, it seemed like his chest rose and fall, so I raised my arm and let off two more rounds in his back.

Boca! Boca!

Blood soaked through the back of his shirt and it was an amazing sight. It was like making my very own tie-dye tee shirt. All of his movements had ceased, so I leaned down to watch him take his very last breath. To stare death in the face was never on my bucket list, but I had to admit, it felt good to take a life. Not in a sense that I wanted to become a serial killer, it was more of a control thing. I got to choose whether he lived or died and I chose death. Control was something I wasn't used to having. For me, I was always the one being controlled but tonight, all of that changed.

"Zuri! Zuri!"

The sound of Brick shouting my name sent a wave of relief over my body. My knight in shining armor had finally arrived and I knew I had nothing further to worry about. I stepped over

156

the body and met him directly in front of the bathroom. We stood face-to-face, before I handed him the gun and threw my arms around his neck.

"Baby, I'm so glad you're here. Don't ever leave me alone again. You don't understand how scared I was in here."

Brick kissed me on top of my head. "I'm sorry, baby. This will never happen again. I promise you that." He let me go and looked at me from head to toe. Then, he rubbed my stomach. "You okay?"

I nodded my head. "Yes. I think Bre is asleep, because she never came out that room."

"Check on her and see." Brick stepped to the side and went into the bathroom.

"You good, sis?" Coop approached me and gave me a hug. He was always sweet and sincere, so I couldn't understand what the issue was between him and that crazy-ass Danielle.

"I am now. Did y'all see anybody outside? There was two of them in here."

"Nah. We didn't even see a squad car outside. So, whoever he came here with, done cleared out on him."

"Aye, bruh, come here real quick." Brick peeked from behind the bathroom wall.

"Sup." Coop stepped into the bathroom with him, so I poked my head in discreetly, just to be nosey.

"Look at this nigga and tell me who this is."

Coop leaned down and shook his head. "Nigga, that's Tyrone. Deja's fuck-ass cousin."

"See, I had to make sure I wasn't fuckin' trippin' in this bitch." Brick leaned up against the wall and ran his hand over his face. "So, that means this silly-ass ho' sent her cousin here to hurt my lady and my fuckin' daughter is here."

"Ion even wanna believe she did no shit like this."

Out of nowhere, Brick turned around and threw a punch. His fist went straight through the dry wall. "I'ma kill this ho', I swear."

"We gone get to the bottom of this shit, but first we gotta get this body out of here." Coop pulled his phone from his back pocket and dialed a number.

"Hello."

"Aye, get the truck and meet me at the location I'm about to send you."

"A'ight. I'm on my way."

When he hung up the phone, Brick was looking crazy. "Bruh, you called Skeet?"

"Yeah. Shit, you want this body out of here, don't you?"

Brick thought for a moment before replying, "I guess you right."

"It ain't like you staying here after this shit went down, so it don't matter if he know where you live right now."

"Facts. I'm on the realtor's ass tomorrow." Brick walked to the doorway and stepped into the hallway. "Did you check on Bre?"

"Um. She's still asleep," I lied. My ass was too busy eavesdropping and I never checked on her.

"Pack a bag, 'cause y'all not staying here."

"You say we not staying, so where are you staying?" I was confused, because if he thought he was staying, he had another thing coming.

"We all going to a hotel, but I gotta clean this place up and break my lease. I'll have the realtor look for a house. I'm done with the apartment shit, so get to packing and we'll discuss this later."

"Okay."

My nigga was right, because he had a lot of explaining to do and on everything I loved, Deja was gone to see me. That ho' put me, her own daughter and my unborn child in grave danger. If I didn't check that bitch, my name wasn't Zuri muthafuckin' Monroe. Sis definitely had me fucked up. Not only that, I'd caught my first body that night and I felt gangsta as fuck. There was no going back because Brick now had me corrupted by a gangsta.

***

Mehzani

There was nothing in the world I wanted more than to have Gucci back at home with me. Now that he was here, I wasn't too sure about that anymore. The love I had for him wasn't the issue, because I loved him from the bottom of my heart. That man was the air I breathed and I knew I couldn't live life without him. He was the reason I was able to kick my drug habit, one hundred percent.

The problem was, I didn't believe I was strong enough to take care of him the way I wanted to and the way he needed me to. Our lack in being unable to communicate with one another is what was killing me and made matters worse. Gucci was the strong one and I didn't want to look like a failure in his eyes. That would probably kill the love he has for me.

My thoughts were really fucking with me and the only thing helping me cope was the Hennessy I was consuming while sitting on the patio.

"Mehzani, you have to stay strong and stand in the paint with the only man that loved you past your pain and addiction. He deserves more than you giving him. You know how it feels to have people walk out your life."

No matter how much of a pep talk I gave myself, it just wasn't working for me. I felt helpless and useless at the same time. Mel wanted to come around, but I wouldn't allow him to be there. My conscience was beating my ass for fucking him while Gucci was in the hospital, and I wasn't ready to face that demon yet. God knows I wanted to tell him so bad while he was in this state. And that was only because I knew if I confessed now, by the time he made a full recovery he would've had time to forgive me for my indiscretion. It wasn't like he hadn't cheated on me and it wasn't like I cheated on some revenge-type shit. I was weak and vulnerable when I thought he was going to die. That night, I needed a shoulder to cry on and a dick to ride to take my mind off of things. At least, that's what the liquor told me.

The night was dark and peaceful, but my silent cries brought on disruption with my sanity. Tears flowed down my face and onto my chest. I felt selfish for only thinking of myself. Now was the time for me to prove I was here for him through thick and thin, but I was failing already. An epiphany popped in my mind and I thought of the one person that could help me and literally talk me off the cliff, so I hit her up.

"What's up, sis?" Zuri sounded like she was moving around.

"I'm going through it and I need some help. But, if you busy, I'll call you back."

"No. It's fine. I'm just getting settled in this damn hotel. Hold on, while I put my step-daughter in the bed."

"Okay."

I could hear Zuri calling Bre's name. My take was that Brick wasn't around, since I didn't hear his voice in the background. From what my sister said, he took pride in putting his baby girl to bed and reading her a bedtime story. That was the type of father I wanted for my child, whenever I had one. Hopefully, that would be me and Gucci whenever his health was back on track.

While I waited for Zuri to come back to the phone, I poured up another cup of Hennessy, because I had a lot to get off my chest. Sus didn't know she was in for a treat. My ass was borderline drunk and overly emotional. I was about to talk her ass to death.

There was some rustling on the other end of the phone, then some heavy breathing. "I'm back."

"You good over there?"

"Yeah. I'm just fat as fuck and out of shape like a bitch. I just want my body back, because I know for a fact my organs tired of being sat on and pushed around."

"I know. I can't wait to see my nephew and hold him. He's going to be so handsome."

"I'm too ready to meet my prince."

"Have you thought of any names yet?"

"No. Not yet and I'm not too thrilled on making him a junior either."

"Why not? What's wrong with Brandon?"

"Nothing. I just don't want him to feel like he needs to live up to his father's name. You know how that goes," Zuri sighed. "Brick is gangsta as fuck and so damn hardcore. I don't want my son to think he has to grow up and be the same way."

"That's very true, so I understand what you saying."

"So, what's going on with my baby sis? How is life treating you?"

"Girl, get comfortable, because I need the prayer warriors solicited for this."

"Oh, Lord," she giggled. "I'm glad Brick not here, so you can have me all to yourself."

"Good." I laughed too and took a deep breath, so I could spill my guts out to her.

***

The next day, I felt like a new woman and I owed it all to my sister. We sat and talked on the phone for two hours. Zuri reassured me everything would be okay and she had my back one hundred percent. It made me feel good that I had a support system to lean on, whenever I felt like shit wasn't going good on my end. The journey I faced wasn't going to be easy, but I was determined to be strong.

In honor of my appreciation, I invited Zuri over for a home-cooked meal. On the menu was curry chicken, cabbage and corn bread. Jamaican food was one of my favorite dishes, so it was only right I whipped that up.

Gucci was lying down on his hospital bed in the living room, watching television. I knew he wouldn't want to be cooped up in that room day in and out, so I chose an area that had more scenery. This way, he could see me while I cooked, cleaned or did laundry. I sat my oven mitts on the counter and walked over to where he was.

"Are you okay, my love?" I kissed him on the cheek and awaited a gesture. Gucci's face balled up like he was questioning my words. Normally, I would get aggravated if he couldn't understand me, but patience was a virtue and something I needed to perfect. Therefore, I took Zuri's advice on communication. Slowly, I reached for Gucci's hand and took it into mine. He was relaxed as he waited for what I was about to do. I placed his hand close to my mouth and kissed it, before placing it on my cheek.

"I know you can hear me, but you have to help me understand you, okay? It may get frustrating, baby, but we will get through this together, I promise. Do you understand what I'm saying?"

Gucci nodded his head.

"I want to apologize to you for getting aggravated with you. The last thing I want is for you to feel as if you are a burden on me, because you aren't. I love you more than life itself and I'll be here until the end of time. I'm going to nurse you back to health, I promise you that. But, you have to want it more than I do. That's the only way you will conquer this."

Gucci didn't move or make a sound. He looked deep into my eyes and I could see his sockets fill up with water. Tears fell from them and God knows I wanted to cry, but I couldn't. Not in front of him. Moving closer to him, I used my right hand to wipe away his tears.

"Please, don't cry. I'm not going anywhere, I promise." It was so hard to contain my emotions while he broke down, so I dropped my head and explained the situation as best as I could.

"Last night, I had a meltdown because I didn't feel like I could take care of you the way you took care of me. You are so much stronger than me and I was weak. It was embarrassing and that was why I drank so much liquor. I called my sister and she was there for me while I cried on the phone for almost two hours. I just don't want to look like a failure in your eyes, and then you leave me when you get well."

Gucci's hand was in my lap at that moment and I could feel him pull away from me. That made my heart sink to the pit of my stomach. To me, that was an indication he was upset with me. When he grabbed my hand and pulled it in his direction that made me look up at him. Following his lead, I moved closer to him at the head of the bed. It was obvious he had upper-body strength by the way he embraced me in his arms. His touch alone still did something to me and I wish we could go further, but I knew there wasn't a snowball's chance in hell his dick would stand up. If it could, I would ride the shit out of him on a daily basis. When he let me go, he held up the "I love you" sign and placed my hand over his heart.

"I love you too."

The knock on the door caught me off guard, causing me to jump out my damn skin. Gucci's head swiveled in the direction of the door. "That's my sister. Remember I said I wanted you to meet her? She's dating your cousin, Brick."

He didn't respond, nor did his facial expression change, so I got up and headed to the door. Once the locks were unsecured, I pulled the door open and Zuri was standing there with a huge smile on her face and a little girl at her side.

"Hey, sis."

"Hey, boo." We hugged each other then she introduced me to her company. "This is Breanna."

I kneeled down to her level and smiled. "Hey, Breanna. It's nice to finally meet you. I'm Zuri's sister, Mehzani."

"Hi. Do you have snacks over here?" She placed her hand on her itty bitty hip.

Zuri and I busted out laughing. "Really, Bre? That's the first thing you ask when you meet someone new?"

Breanna shrugged her shoulders. "Well, she is your sister, right?"

"Oh my, you are a mess." I laughed again. "That's fine. I'm your auntie now, okay?"

"Chi, that's a grown lady," Zuri agreed.

"Okay. Take me to the snacks then." Breanna grabbed my hand and walked inside the condo. Zuri closed the door and followed behind us.

As we approached Gucci's bed, Breanna let go of my hand and took off running. "Uncle Gucci. Uncle Gucci."

The sight of his niece lit up his eyes and a joyful smile spread across his lips. For the first time since he'd been home, he leaned up. And then, he hugged her.

"I miss you," she whispered. Breanna tilted her head to the side for a few seconds. When he didn't reply, she looked at him and frowned. "Why won't you talk to me?"

Immediately, I rushed over and placed my hand on her shoulder. "Umm. Bre, Uncle Gucci is not able to talk to you right now, because he's sick. When he's better, he'll be able to talk to you, okay?"

"Okay."

"But he misses you too."

"How do you know?" she asked.

"I'll show you. Turn around." I turned her back in the direction of her uncle to prove to her what I already knew. "Baby, do you miss Breanna?" He nodded his head yes and that made her smile.

My sister walked up and stood beside me. "Baby, this is my sister, Zuri."

"We met before." Zuri smiled. "Hi, Gucci, I'm happy to see you out of the hospital and doing better. My sister is going to take good care of you, so you're in good hands."

The front door slammed and we all looked over with the quickness to see who had just walked in. Brick scrolled in with his hands in his pockets and a grin on his face. "What's up, Cuz? How you feeling these days?"

At that moment, Gucci's eyes protruded from their sockets like golf balls, and his body shook hard like a knocking transmission. I had never witnessed that type of behavior from him and I was scared out my mind. He rocked back and forth uncontrollably with his eyes closed.

"He's having a seizure. Call 911," Zuri shouted.

Chapter 17

Zuri

A few days had passed since we visited my sister and Gucci had that episode. After the paramedics came to pick him up, we left. Needless to say we never had dinner and Brick had been silent about the whole ordeal, but that was about to change. The hospital ran multiple tests on him and concluded he did not have a seizure, but a panic attack instead. That meant one thing in my eyes. Gucci felt like he was in danger. Mehzani also confirmed she had never witnessed that type of behavior from him before. Now, I wasn't a psychic or no shit like that, but my intuition was telling me Brick was responsible for what happened to his own cousin, and I wasn't going to rest until he told me the absolute truth.

"So, are you going to tell me why your cousin spazzed out like that the moment he saw you?"

Brick acted as if he was so into packing up the boxes that he didn't hear me. Breanna was upstairs in my bedroom watching television, so it was the perfect time to bring it up.

"Brandon!" I called his name loudly. "I know you hear me talking to you."

He took his eyes off the box and focused on me. "I didn't hear you, baby. What's up?"

"Why did Gucci react that way when he saw you?"

Brick shrugged his shoulders. "How am I supposed to know? I'm not a doctor."

"Don't get smart with me." I threw the tape on the floor. "You know exactly what I'm talking about. So again, what did you do to him?"

"Like I told you the other day, I ain't do shit to him. I don't know why you don't believe me." Brick was trying his best to convince me otherwise, but I wasn't going for the okey-doke. He had to wake up early in the morning to pull a fast one on me.

"And like I told you before, I was born at night, not last night." I walked over to where he was and sat down on the sofa. "So, this what it all boils down to, you lying to me now? The Brick I know would never do that."

Brick gave me the side eye and smirked. It was that same devious smirk he had when he walked into Gucci's place. "Sarcasm won't get you very far with me, and reverse psychology won't work, point-blank, period. I wrote the book on that shit."

"I'm not sarcastic. I'm too intelligent beyond your understanding."

"Keep thinking that."

"I see you take me for an absolute fool." I looked up at the stairway to make sure Bre hadn't wandered out the room. Since the coast was clear, I made sure to keep my voice at a minimum. "Did you forget I'm well aware of you going to see him that night? The same night we went to Deja's house?"

"Zuri, drop it, okay?"

"No. I'm not dropping shit until you tell me what happened."

Brick stopped packing, dropped the tape he was holding onto the floor and did an about-face in my direction. "Why you steady going on about this? You trying to piss me off, huh?"

"No I'm not. I just want the truth."

On any other occasion, I would've stopped the moment the veins popped out his head, but I promised my sister that I would see if Brick knew anything about Gucci's shooting. Based on the way our conversation was going, I was pretty certain that I had my answer. All I wanted was a confession.

Three steps later, he was standing in front of me. "There is no fuckin' truth, so stop questioning me about my business. You too goddamn nosey for your own good."

"Why you getting so mad?" I leaned back on the sofa and crossed my legs. "Must be true, if you running up on me like you want to hit me."

"Nah, you keep jugging and I done told you to mind your own business. This family business and it has nothing to do with you, plain and simple."

The baby started to move, so I rubbed my stomach with a look of discomfort on my face. Immediately, I assumed it was because of all the noise. "You okay?" he asked.

"The baby moving, that's all."

Brick got down on his knees and rubbed my stomach. "Why every time we argue, the first thing you assume is I'm about to hit you?"

"Because you get so upset and too close."

"So, why poke the bear if you know this already?"

"You lying to me and I don't like it."

"Believe me when I say you could never survive a hit from me. I know my strength and that's why I'll never put my hands on you. One thing I don't want to see is my woman walking around with black eyes and a busted lip, because I couldn't control myself."

Brick was right. An abusive relationship wasn't what I wanted. "I'm sorry, baby. I just got so caught up with everything my sister's going through. She just wants to know what happened to him."

"The streets are a dangerous place. Especially when it comes down to the line of work we're involved in. Your enemies could be your closest partners and family members."

The doorbell rang.

"I got it." Brick got up and went to the door. "Who is it?"

"I have a delivery."

Brick peeped through the glass before he opened the door. It was a young guy dressed in a UPS uniform. "What's up?"

"I have a delivery for Zuri Monroe."

"Where do I sign?" The guy handed him the clipboard, then eventually, a vase of roses and a box. "Thanks, man," he replied and kicked the door closed behind him. I got up and waddled towards the door and locked it.

Brick allowed the box to fall on the sofa and paid special attention to the roses. "Who the hell sending you flowers?"

My ass was clueless, but something was telling me that it was Daman. "I don't know. Maybe my donor."

He stuck his hand inside and found a card. As he read it, I could see his pupils moving back and forth, but then he stopped. "So, you mean to tell me you still talking to this nigga?"

The boom in his voice made me so nervous, I was trembling. "What are you talking about? I'm not talking to anyone."

Brick looked back down at the card. "Zuri, I'm sorry about the other day. I hope this grand gesture makes up for it. I also sent you something for the baby. The roses symbolize my feelings towards you. Jason."

This fool was trying to get me killed with his dumb ass. He knew damn well Brick was gone see this shit, which made me feel as though he was trying to cause problems in my relationship. The look on Brick's face was similar to the day he caught me on lunch and made me quit my job. I started praying silently for him to calm down.

"So, you still talking to this nigga?" Brick walked casually towards me, but I was taking baby steps backwards.

"No." I shook my head from side to side.

"So, why the fuck he keep reaching out to you?" He had that vase clutched tight as hell.

"I keep telling you that we were friends for years."

"You fucked that nigga."

"No, I didn't," I shouted in my defense.

"You a muthafuckin' lie." Brick cocked back and threw the vase against the wall, causing it to shatter. Glass, water, and rose petals went flying all over the place.

I was terrified when he stepped to me, with his fist balled up and breathing heavily. "You must think I'm fuckin' stupid."

"I didn't do anything," I screamed, with a face full of tears.

Brick was on one thousand and I knew he was about to do some damage to me. It hadn't been long since he gave me a warning of how badly he could fuck me up with no effort.

My life flashed before my eyes and all I could see were knuckles coming in my direction. Brick threw a punch and as bad as I wanted to duck, I couldn't. My body was too stiff to move, but nothing. That nigga was swift when he moved. By the grace of God, he missed me by an inch and his fist went crashing into the wall.

"Stop fuckin' playing with me before I hurt you. I'm trying to be so patient with you, but you pushing it."

"Brick," I sniffled. "Baby, I swear, I'm not doing anything and you should know that by now. You have to trust me. I'm nothing like Deja."

"Daddy." When we looked to the right, Breanna was standing beside us rubbing her eyes. "Are you fighting?"

Brick wiped the sweat and tears from his face with his shirt before he turned to face his daughter. Breanna reached for him, so he picked her up. "Daddy, you have to be nice to Zuri. Don't make her cry," she whispered and hugged his neck.

"I won't, baby." Brick then looked at me with sorrowful eyes. "I'm sorry, baby."

When he reached out to me, I stepped into his arms and whispered. "I forgive you, baby."

We stood in that one spot for a few minutes, just embracing one another. That moment was special to me, because I knew he would never put his hands on me. Any other man probably would've beat my ass. But, not Brick, he was a different breed. After this incident, I was severing all ties with Jason and that meant changing my number so he couldn't contact me. Over the years, we've had a good friendship but clearly, he didn't respect boundaries or my relationship, and I wasn't about to lose my family over him.

The knock on the door brought our hugging session to a close. "I'll get it."

Before I opened the door, I wiped the tears from my face and got myself together. I didn't know who to expect, but I was hoping it wasn't another blitz attack. To my surprise, standing on the other side of the door was Shakira, my brother's fiancée and my nephew, Legend Jr. Her presence really took me by surprise. She was the last person I expected to see standing on my porch.

"Shakira," I smiled. "What are you doing here?"

"I have something for you. May I come in?"

"Sure." Shakira took a step towards me and we hugged one another. "It's so good to see you."

"Wow! You're pregnant," she gasped.

"Yeah, I am," I rubbed my stomach. "I didn't get a chance to tell Legend about it before he passed." The mention of his name caused her to go silent and her shoulders to tense up.

My nephew was every spit of my brother and it was so weird looking at his twin in the flesh. Although Legend was gone, we had a little reminder right here on earth. "Hey, nephew. You are so handsome. Come give Auntie a hug."

Legend Jr. took baby steps towards me and gave me a hug. "Hi, Auntie."

"Come in and have a seat." I closed the door and escorted them to the living room area. Brick was still standing in place with Breanna in his arms.

"Baby, this is Shakira, my brother Legend's fiancée, and their son, Legend Jr."

"Nice to meet you," Brick replied. "Baby, I'm going upstairs so you can talk in private."

"Okay."

Shakira sat down and Legend got comfortable, by snuggling underneath his mother in the seat beside her. The last time we were in the same room, it seemed like she was holding it together, but not today. Her eyes had bags underneath them, like she hadn't slept in months and could carry a ton of grocery bags in them. It was obvious she lost a lot of weight, so that explained why her clothes were baggy on her slender frame. My mind could only imagine the pain she was feeling after losing the love of her life to gun violence.

"How have you been?"

"Not good, Zuri. These last few months have been hell for me. I haven't been able to eat or sleep since I went back to Carolina."

"I know how you feel. I've been going through it myself."

Shakira opened up her purse and pulled out a box of Kleenex. Taking out a few pieces, she dabbed her eyes and turned her attention back to me. "Life, as I know it to be is over, and I swear I want to give up."

The words that fell from her lips were not something I thought L.J. should be listening to. "Hold on. I'm going to send L.J. upstairs so we can talk in peace."

"Okay." Shakira blew her nose while I got up and escorted L.J. to the stairs. "Baby, come here please," I screamed.

Brick surfaced from the bedroom and stood at the top of the stairs. "Can you keep him up there until finish talking please?"

"Send him up."

"L.J., go upstairs with Uncle Brick and I'll call you when you can come back, okay handsome?"

Legend Jr. nodded his head and went upstairs.

"Now that he's gone, let me say this." Instead of sitting in my seat, I decided to sit beside her. "Shakira, you've been in this family since we were younger and you know I love you like a sister."

"I know," she replied.

"It hurts me to see you like this, without me being able to do anything to comfort you or make the pain go away. I know for a fact you loved my brother."

"I do, Z, and I will never love another man like that. I know for a fact that will never happen. Legend was everything to me. That's who I lost my virginity to. That's the man I chose to father my children and now he's gone."

"Shakira, you said children. What do you mean by that?"

She started to sob loudly and rock back and forth. I remained silent and allowed her to calm herself down. Finally she spoke. "I'm pregnant and now, my baby will never get the chance to meet her father. Life just ain't fair. He didn't fuck with nobody. Why me? Why my family?"

Our pain was the same, so watching her break down made me do the same. Reaching over, I hugged and squeezed her tight. "Those are my same questions, but we will never get that closure. They still haven't made an arrest and that's the part that's killing me."

"I miss him so much that I want to go with him. There were so many times I've thought about taking my own life, but when I look into my baby's eyes, I know I can't leave him alone in this world. He already doesn't have a father, what would that do for him if I killed myself?"

"You can't do that. He needs you more than ever now." Shakira needed to look in my eyes when I said these next words to her, so I released the hold I had on her. Hopefully, it would make her see things in a different light.

"Listen, we are going to get through this together. Whatever you need, I'm here for you. If you need a break from L.J., I got him. All you have to do is let me know. That's what I'm here for."

Shakira nodded her head. "I need you now more than ever. My baby sees me cry every single day and that's not healthy for a child."

She wiped her face with her tissue and held it in her hand. "The other day, he saw me crying and he said, 'Mommy, do you miss Daddy?' It hurt me to the depth of my soul to tell him yes and that he's never coming home again."

"What do you need me to do?" I asked.

"Can you watch L.J. for a few days, so I can get my thoughts together? My mom wants me to move back to Lauderdale. I don't want to, but I can't live in that house without him. He relocated us so we could raise our kids in a different environment from the one we grew up in."

"Of course, I'll watch my nephew. That's not a problem."

"Thank you so much. I'm going to start seeing a counselor, so I can start my healing process. L.J. will be in a world of trouble if I don't get the help that I need."

"Do what you need to do so you can be the strong mother he needs you to be."

"I also have this for you." Shakira slipped her hand inside her bag and pulled out an envelope. "This is from Legend. A few months before he died, he had this drawn up just in case something happened to him."

"What is it?" I was skeptical as I took the envelope from her.

"Open it."

For some reason, I was nervous and I didn't know why. My hands trembled as I struggled to get it open. When I finally tore it open, I pulled out the letter and began to read it. Apparently, Legend had a will and he left both Mehzani and me one hundred thousand dollars each. The letter was a total shocker, because I would've never expected anything from him

"Wow! I don't know what to say."

"Don't say anything. He always told me it was his responsibility to make sure his sisters were taken care of, even in death."

Shakira's phone rang. She looked at the screen and put it back inside her purse. "That's my mom. I have to go, so I can get ready to meet the psychiatrist."

"Okay."

"Can you get Legend for me?"

I walked to the stairs and shouted his name. "Legend, come here. Your mom wants you."

Seconds later, my nephew came flying down the steps like a bat out of hell and straight into his mother's arms. "You're going to stay with Auntie for a few days and I'll be back to pick you up, okay?"

"You promise?" His voice was so soft.

"I promise, baby. Mommy needs to get help so she can stop crying all the time. Be a big boy for Mommy while I'm gone."

"I will, Mommy."

Shakira hugged him tight. "Legend, I love you so much. I swear to God I do, and don't you ever forget that."

"I love you too, Mommy," he said sweetly.

"I have to get you his bag out the car. I'll be right back."

"Alright." When the door closed, Brick came downstairs. He looked at Legend, then back at me. "What's going on?"

"Um. Legend, baby, you can go back upstairs and watch television while Auntie talks to your uncle." Legend was as obedient as they came. He trotted back upstairs with no problem.

"She needs me to keep him for a few days, while she goes to counseling and get situated with the move back here."

"Oh, okay." Brick hugged me and kissed my forehead. "You okay?"

"Yes. I'm okay."

Shakira walked back inside, toting a small duffle bag. "Thank you so much, Zuri. I'll see you in a few days."

"That's what family is for. Come here." We hugged once more.

"You don't know how much I appreciate this." She pulled back and wiped her eyes. "Take care of my baby. He's all we have left."

"Don't worry. My nephew is in good hands."

When Shakira left, Brick and I went back to packing up my belongings to put in storage, until we found a house. Taking care of two kids was going to be quite interesting, but I was up to the task. Although shit was crazy for us, helping those in need was important to me, and I was going to hold my brother's family down by any means necessary. I owed him that much.

Chapter 18

Daman

One week later

Solitary confinement was just another way for me to sit back and analyze shit for what it really was. I spent so much time in that muthafucka that I wasn't fazed one bit. To pass the time, I did a lot of push-ups and boxing. As time continued to pass, I lost track of the days. Normally, Cee would've been down to check on me, but he'd been MIA. The flap on my cell opened and the lights from the hallway shined on the inside.

"Shower time," the C.O. hollered before unlocking the door.

"It's about damn time. A nigga ain't showered in three muthafuckin' days."

"The proper response is, thanks for coming down and letting me wash my funky ass," the C.O. replied with a slight chuckle.

"Ya' mama ain't think I was funky when she had a mouth full of this dick." I grabbed my crotch, stepped out my cell and looked him up and down. "Y'all young niggas got the game fucked up. I'll knock yo' ass out in this bitch. Now, let's go so I can wash these gorilla nuts."

The officer closed his mouth and escorted me to the shower and unlocked the door. Once I was on the inside, he turned his back to me. "You got fifteen minutes."

"Whateva!" I huffed and removed my shirt. After discarding all my clothing, I hung it up on the metal hook.

Nobody told me how long I would be in this bitch, but they was gone get me out of here. All I needed was my phone, so I could hit the warden up and let him know what his ingrates were up to. If he wasn't on vacation, I would've been out the box, but it was all good. My day was coming.

The hot water felt so good splashing all over my body. I just knew the little bit of time he hollering about wasn't gone be enough for me to handle my business. Shit, a nigga was trying to beat. Instead of doing what I wanted, I washed my ass first, just in case he came back too goddamn fast for me. My eyes were closed tight while I rinsed the suds from my chest.

"Arghh!" A sharp piercing pain erupted in my side, which caused me to flinch and grab my side. "What the fuck?"

When I turned around, Cee was standing inside the shower stall with me, holding a shank. "Nigga what the fuck you doing?" The pain in my side stung like a muthafucka.

"I gotta take you out, man," he replied calmly.

"Fuck you mean?"

Cee rushed me, swinging his arm trying to finish me off, but I jumped back and put my set up, before throwing two punches at him. Both of my fists connected with his face, rocking his head like a bobble head. Cee didn't stop though, he continued to take jabs at me, but he missed. It was do or die at that point. The pain in my side became numb as my adrenaline pumped hard. With all the strength in me, I rushed him and his back collided with the wall. His arm fell at his side and I was able to grab it, while disarming him of his weapon. We both knew he couldn't beat me if we fought head-up, and that's why he tried that blitz attack bullshit.

The shank was now gripped tightly in my right hand and my left forearm was pressed hard against his throat. "Fuck nigga, I did all this shit for you and this how you repay me, bitch?"

Rapidly, my hand jammed the shank into his stomach. His warm blood from his wound spilled out onto my hand, but that didn't stop me from making multiple holes in his stomach. Cee's eyes were wide open and so was his mouth. The blood coming from his mouth leaked out onto his shirt. For the final stab, I rammed it deep into his open stomach and held it there. Our eyes locked and I could feel the air from his mouth on my face. His breathing was shallow, so I knew death was near. As I waited patiently, he finally took his final breath. Then, I yanked the shank from his stomach and lowered his body to the floor.

"You stupid muthafucka. Thought you could kill me? You got the game fucked up too. Yo' ass better hope I don't kill ya' mama when I get out for raising a fuck nigga."

That son of a bitch really tried me, so I kicked him one time for good measure. I knew the officer would be coming soon, so I showered again to get the blood off of me. My body looked like I just got finished smashing a virgin and shit got real nasty. Blood continue to spill from my wound, so I allowed the water to clean it.

"Goddamn it. This shit hurt like a muthafucka."

"Aye, shower time is up," the C.O shouted and tapped on the door before opening it. He saw Cee's body on the floor. "What the fuck happened in here?"

"Fuck it look like, nigga? This bitch tried to kill me."

"How do I know that?" His young ass was acting mighty tough, like he was untouchable.

"'Cause this bitch not supposed to be down here, but something telling me I should ask you how the fuck he got in here."

The officer leaned against the door and folded his arms. "Nah, I'm asking all the questions and if you don't answer correctly, I'll testify in court, saying I witnessed you attack the victim."

"So what you saying?"

"I'm saying, I need twenty bands to keep me from singing like a bird and if not," he shrugged his shoulders. "You can use that same money to beat this new murder charge."

A murder charge is something I couldn't afford to get. I knew it was self-defense, but that would be hard to prove during a trial. Ain't this a bitch? This bitch boy was trying to extort me for money in order for him to remain silent. I scratched my head and nodded.

"Cool. You got it."

"I'll get the info on where to send it. You have until tomorrow to get my money."

"No problem." That was the way the cookie crumbled, so I sucked it up and grabbed my towel from the hook. "I need to get dressed."

"Hurry up, so I can call someone down here to clean this shit up."

Bitch Boy turned his back to me and that was when I threw the towel over his head and snatched him back into the shower with me. His arms swung aimlessly, but I had him gripped too tight.

"Bitch, I told you don't fuck with me." I slammed his head into the wall.

After doing that repeatedly, I heard his skull crack and he finally stopped moving. Immediately, I dropped his body onto the floor and stepped from the shower. My first mind was to get dressed, but I needed proof that I was caught off-guard. But before I left, I ran through their pockets. The officer had some cash, so I took that shit. Cee had my cellphone in his pocket. That was a no-brainer. I was about to get in touch with the free world. After cuffing the phone, I rushed to the main door and started beating on it.

"Aye! Open this muthafuckin' door. I got an emergency down here. Yooo! People dead down here, muthafuckas."

Surprisingly, it didn't take long for someone to come to the door. I stepped back so the female officer could come in. When she crossed the threshold, she looked me up and down. "Mm. What's going on back here? And why you bleeding?"

"One of the inmates tried to stab me and the officer tried to stop him. They started fighting and I ran. Both of they asses dead in the shower."

"Alright. Go to your cell and get dressed. I'll have transport take you to the hospital. In the meantime, continue to apply pressure to that wound."

"Yeah."

Inside my cell, I scrolled through the phone to see who this nigga been talking to. Apparently, he been talking to someone, in order for him to come at me like that. Whoever was behind it better count they muthafuckin' days, because I was coming hard.

"Damn this nigga had everybody and they mammie calling my shit. That's why he couldn't get his ass down here and…"

The sleeve of text messages that caught me off-guard came from Zuri. Their conversation caused my heart rate to increase. It felt like a nigga chest was about to explode from a broken heart. She was really speaking with this nigga about me. My eyes moved quickly across the thread and I froze. There was no way I was reading it correctly. I sent a quick text, just to confirm.

Zuri: Aye, let Brick know I handled that for him
Don't Answer: Okay

Now I was looking stupid. Zuri knew I didn't like the nigga, so there was no way she thought it was me and him talking. My conscience was fucking with me bad and I couldn't keep quiet, so I hit her up.

"Hello."

"Wow! I'm surprised you picked up. Last time we spoke you told me you would never talk to me again in life."

"Well, you got me, so now what?" Zuri was busted and her ass still had an attitude.

There was only one conclusion. She was down for the cause. It was difficult to keep my cool, but I kept that shit G. "So, that's how you get down now? You had this nigga try and kill me."

"What are you talking about?" Zuri tried to remain calm, but I could hear the shakiness in her voice.

"Don't act dumb. You know exactly what I'm talm 'bout."

"I don't know shit," she snapped.

"Damn, it's like that? I can't believe that after all we been through, you would go against the grain like that. How you let a nigga in your life and allow him to turn you against me?"

"Oh, you mean the way you put a hit out on the father of my child? Or the fact that you hired someone to harm me, so I can lose my baby?"

"Zuri, you already know I love you and I'll never let you walk away from me. Right now, you acting stupid and naïve, so you not thinking straight."

"Fuck you and I hope you die in that bitch. I hate you and everything you stand for. I wish I would've left you to rot alone a long time ago, you sick and twisted bastard."

That was the worst shit she ever said to me, but I couldn't let my emotions get the best of me. Before I really went there, I inhaled deeply and released it slowly.

"I'm going to ignore the stupid shit you just said, because we both know how this relationship started. It was you. You cried and cried, until I became intimate with you. That wasn't something I would've chosen to do, but I didn't want to hurt your feelings anymore so I gave in and now, I'm locked up for some shit that you wanted. Keep in mind, I will be free one day and I will remember this conversation. And I will see you."

"You may be getting out, but you'll never see me again in life, and that's a promise."

"I wouldn't be so sure about that. I'm going to appear when you least expect it. Mark my words."

"Anyway, I'm hanging up, so you can miss me with that."

"Before you go, let ya' baby daddy know his plan to kill me failed and his homeboy, Cee, is dead. Tell that nigga to count his muthafuckin' days."

Zuri ended the call, but I didn't care. She heard what the fuck I said and nothing further needed to be addressed. Both of them would be seeing me sooner or later.

***

Brick

Coop and I stood on the side of the shop building in the grassy area, waiting on the transport truck to pull all the way in with the vehicles.

"Damn, bruh, this was a dope ass idea. Now, these boys can ride late night with no problems," Coop rubbed his hands together. "Hell yeah! We in the money now."

"That's cause I'm that nigga with the masterplan. We 'bouta eat lovely round this bitch. Prison ain't teach a nigga shit, but how to be a better criminal. The ins and outs and how to stay free. One of my cellies was in the mob, so he taught me some shit."

"All we gotta do is keep moving in silence and when we have this bitch on lock, we can kick back. After that, it's vacation time with the family."

"Yeah, I'm looking forward to those family vacations and shit. Zuri gone love that shit."

"You already know, bruh-bruh."

"Get ready to retire early, my nigga." I walked off and met the driver at his truck. A big black dude jumped down and shook my hand.

"Are you Brandon Riccardo?"

"That would be me," I replied.

"Good. I just need you to sign right here." He handed me a clipboard. "You want the cars closer to the fence?"

"Just drop 'em wherever. I'll move 'em."

"These are the keys to all of them." The driver passed me an envelope.

"Thanks."

"You're welcome." The driver tossed the clipboard through the window of the truck and walked to the back and started to unload each vehicle.

While I waited on him to unload the vehicles, I decided to check up on Zuri and Breanna. The phone rang a long time before she finally picked up.

"Hey."

"What you doing?"

"Nothing."

"Well, why it took you so long to answer the phone?" It never took her long to pick up whenever I called if she was doing nothing. Not to mention, her response was dry, so I knew something was wrong.

"No reason."

"Okay, what's going on? Because I know something is wrong and don't tell me nothing. I know better than that."

Zuri was silent at first, but then I heard a sniffle.

"Zuri, are you crying? What's wrong?"

There was more hesitation, followed by more sniffles. Then, she finally spoke up. "Daman called me today."

"What did he say?"

"He knows you set him up to be killed, but your plan failed. Then he said your friend, Cee, is dead." Zuri started to whimper and I wished I was there to intercept that call. "You didn't tell me you were going to have him killed."

"I know, but it was for a good reason. You shouldn't be stressing about nothing. It's my responsibility to take care of you and make sure you okay. Don't let Daman get in your head. Did you forget he hired somebody to kill me and hurt you?"

The last thing I needed right now was for her to have a meltdown over someone that couldn't care less about her or our child. Daman crossed the muthafuckin' line and he was gone suffer dearly. It didn't matter if I had to wait two or three years to touch him. That shit was happening by any means. Time didn't mean shit to me and if Zuri knew any better, she'd better start mourning his ass now. I was gone kill Daman and that was my word.

"I'll be home soon and we can talk about it when I get there."

"Okay," she replied before hanging up.

Once the call was over, I looked up to see the driver had unloaded all of the vehicles and was backing out. He hit the horn and waved from the window. I chucked up the deuces and walked over to where Coop was standing.

"Squad here."

"A'ight. This gone be quick, 'cause I gotta get home."

"Me too."

Inside the break room, the Brick Money Boyz were all seated, focused on me and prepared, just the way I like it. There were still six of us and that's because Kamari took Tone's place. Coop stood at the front with me.

"Everybody on time and paying attention. I like that." I reached into my pockets and pulled out a wad of cash. After I counted off twelve hundred dollars, I shoved the rest back into my pocket.

"Take two hundred dollars and pass the rest around." I handed the money to Chris, since he was sitting in the front.

"Oh, that's what's up, Boss," he chuckled and passed the rest of the money off. "We got a bonus."

"It's not much, but I just want to show my appreciation for everyone doing what's expected. That's how a riff is created, when one in the bunch doesn't feel appreciated. We're more than dealers, we share a brotherhood and I want everyone to be treated as such. Now, as you all know by now, Kamari is the newest in the bunch. He took Tone's place, so show him the same love."

Out of nowhere, my mind went back to Zuri and the slight conversation we had. Whenever I got like that, it made it hard for me to focus, knowing she was hurting. "This meeting is gone be short, 'cause I have to go, but Coop is gone fill y'all in on some new shit we got going on."

I sat down and gave Coop the floor. While he spoke, I shot Zuri a quick text.

Husband: I love you and I'm on my way.
Wifey: Okay

"We'll be moving product differently now. We just had a total of ten taxicabs come in and that's the way you'll be moving going forward. That takes the heat off of you, so you can hustle in peace."

The squad nodded their heads and made comments of approval. "Oh shit, we got company cars now." Chris laughed.

"Damn right. So, if y'all fuck up my car, you bought it and I'm getting my cash off the top," I added.

"We have shirts for you to wear to make it look legit and professional. All we ask is that you be smart. We haven't had any problems up to now, so this is just a forewarning. Leave your shirts in the lockers, so you don't have to worry about leaving them at home."

"So, what if somebody want a ride?" Chris was very talkative in this meeting. At least he wasn't drunk this time, 'cause he would've been fined.

"Cut on the meter and give they ass a ride," Coop laughed.

"I'm for real, bruh." Chris folded his arms over his chest and sat back. "Shit, I might be short on cash that day."

Coop shook his head. "Nigga, I'm being for real. These are real cabs. Just be smart about who you pick up, though. Ya' ass don't wanna be robbed."

"That fie stay ready like Freddy." Chris smirked.

"Good. Now, do anybody else have any questions before we clear it?" Coop picked up the box of shirts from the floor.

Kamari raised his hand. "I don't have a license."

"For now, you ride with Skeet until I get that taken care of for you." I stood up and fixed my shirt. "I'm out. I gotta get home to my lady and the babies. See y'all boys tomorrow."

"A'ight, Bossman," they all replied individually.

It was time for me to get home and see what the hell Daman's bitch ass put in her head. Cee fucked this up big-time. That nigga was supposed to be in the morgue right about now and all of our problems was supposed to be over. After the unsuccessful hit, I knew this was only the beginning of a war I didn't need.

Chapter 19

Brick

When I made it back to the hotel, Zuri was lying in bed, snuggled up with both of the kids. They were watching a children's movie. I walked in and stood beside her, but she didn't move. So, I grabbed her foot.

"So, nobody see me standing here."

"Hi, Daddy, we watching a movie. You want to watch it with us?" Breanna's eyes stayed on the television.

"Hey. I didn't hear you come in." Zuri glanced at me.

"Hi, Uncle Brick." Legend Jr. looked at me for a split second before going back to the movie.

"What's up, nephew? You been keeping an eye on these ladies for me?"

"Yeah." Just looking at him made me feel worse for what I did. I was the reason he was about to grow up without a father. All I could do was shake my head.

"Zuri, we need to talk." I reached for her hand and pulled her from the bed.

"I'll be right back, babies."

Zuri walked off and I followed. The baby was making her gain weight in all the right places. That ass was getting fatter, along with her breasts. It jiggled as she wobbled to the room. I slid up behind her and grabbed her waist so she could feel my hard dick.

"Damn, bae, yo' ass getting fat." I nibbled on her ear to try and clear her mind. "I'm hitting all this tonight."

"I'm sleepy."

"Sleepy my ass. I'm getting some tonight. You went to sleep on my ass last night, so you should be well-rested."

Zuri flopped down on the bed and left me hanging. "What do you wanna talk about?"

Since she wanted to get straight to the point and ignore my needs, I went for it. "What all did Daman say to you? I know you didn't tell me everything."

Zuri rubbed her hands on her thighs and sighed. She didn't give me any eye contact. "He said, he's not letting me go and I will see him when he gets out. Then, he told me to tell you to count yo' fuckin' days."

When she finally looked up at me, there were tears in her eyes and she looked worried. "He's going to try and kill both of us."

I could tell his words hurt her and now she was worried, but there was no way in hell I was gone let that happen. Daman thought he was bad because Cee fucked up and got killed. That wasn't happening. Whenever he got out, he better count his own muthafuckin' days, 'cause dude was getting bodied and I put that on my dead mama's grave. Grabbing her hands, I placed them to my mouth and kissed them.

"Do you really think I would let him harm you? Come on, you smarter than that. Daman ain't got no clout and I don't see him, period. His attempt to kill me failed."

Zuri looked away like she didn't believe me or some shit. Whatever he said to her made her question my ability to handle business like a man. Gently, I used my hand to turn her head towards me.

"Listen to me, I promise I won't let anything happen to you."

Tears slid from her eyes and down her puffy cheeks. "He's dangerous on the outside. You should've heard him. He meant what he said and I believe him."

"Nah, I'm dangerous and you know that. Well, you only know a portion, but if only you knew how I really got down, you wouldn't be in here crying." I planted a soft kiss on her lips and wiped her eyes. "Stop doubting me, 'cause I promise he can't stand in the paint with me."

"Okay." She nodded her head.

"You good now?"

"Yes."

"Do you trust me with your life?" I needed to be sure about my next move.

"Yes." She nodded once more.

"Do you love me?"

"You know I do."

"I need to hear it though."

She grabbed my face with both hands and smiled. "I love you more than life itself." Then she kissed me aggressively, while moving my hand in between her legs.

"I love you too." I mumbled while our lips were still connected. My dick was throbbing hard as fuck, so I pulled away. "Hold on."

"What? Why you stop?" She pouted.

"Hold on for a second." I got up and went to the bathroom. A few weeks ago, I'd bought her a gift and it was the perfect time to give it to her so she would feel safe and secure with me. I grabbed the box from my bag and went back to the bed.

"Close your eyes and cup your hands together," I instructed. "I have something I want you to feel."

Zuri smiled. "Is it another sex toy, nasty?"

"I guess you'll see when you feel it." Zuri closed her eyes and opened her hands with the palms facing up. Gently, I sat the box in it. "Open your eyes."

When she opened them, I was on one knee. Her eyes dropped down on the satin box in her hand and they started to tremble. "Zuri, I love you and I can't picture life without you. Will you marry me?"

"Are you serious?" she gasped.

"Yes," I chuckled. "I'm not on my knee for nothing."

"Yes, baby. Of course, I will marry you."

That was the answer I was hoping for, so I grabbed the box and removed the three carat, round cut, pave-style engagement ring and slipped it onto her finger. Love was certainly in the air that night, so I pulled my baby up gently by the arms. Our height difference didn't allow us to meet at eye level, but I met my baby halfway. Passionately, I kissed her lips while I removed the shirt she was wearing. The sight of her lifeline going up her round belly put a smile on my face. A woman carrying a child was the most beautiful thing in the world and I knew I chose the right woman to be the mother of my second child and to be my wife.

"I love you so much." I got down on my knees and kissed her stomach, before I pulled down her pajama pants.

"I love you too," she whispered.

Zuri could barely see her pussy, so she made sure she kept up with her Brazilian wax appointments. The fresh scent tickled my nose the closer I got to her spot and licked the center. On contact, she placed her hand on the top of my head, preparing for what was about to come. Slowly, I rolled my tongue up, down and between her lips. It was warm and wet, just the way I liked it.

"Mm." She tossed her head back and pulled my ear.

Using my finger, I pushed her pretty flaps apart and sucked on her clit. Zuri couldn't resist pushing her pussy against my face. While my mouth devoured her peach, I could feel her legs tremble.

"Ss. Baby," she moaned. "You making me weak."

To keep her from collapsing on me, I stopped and scooped her up in the air, then placed her onto the bed. At a fast pace, I removed my clothes. My dick was anxious to get a wet, tight massage. Zuri didn't hesitate to bust it open.

"I see I ain't the only one that's ready."

On my knees, I eased closer to her and guided my dick inside until it disappeared. At a slow tempo, I made passionate love to her. The comfort she felt was beneficial for my child as well. I wasn't trying to give my baby a headache by shaking up his place of residence. Staring at Zuri's face kept me aroused. The way she bit down on her full lips with her eyes closed and moaned so sweetly made me wanna fuck all night. Ain't no telling how many babies she was about to have, 'cause I couldn't pull out if I wanted to. Condoms were definitely out of the question and she sure as hell wasn't getting an abortion. Her body belonged to me and what I said was gone go.

One hour later, we were snuggled underneath one another while *Martin* played on the television screen. Every episode, we laughed like we had never seen the show a day in our lives. There were some things that money couldn't buy and our bond was one of them. Throughout my five-year bid, I never imagined I would come home and find my goddess. God had a great sense of humor and it made me wonder what would've happened to me, if I'd never ran into her the way I did. I guess I'd never know, so I closed my eyes and held my future wife tight. In my heart, I knew I owed her the world and she was about to get it. Zuri was the reason I was alive and free. Technically, I owed her my life.

***

Zuri

The next day, I was awakened by bright lights. When I rolled over Brick was no longer next to me. I stretched my arm over to his side and his spot was cold to the touch. That meant he had been out of bed for a while.

"I know he didn't leave here without telling me?" I mumbled.

Brick was notorious for creeping out the bed while I was still sleeping. And, for the life of me, I can't understand how I don't feel him move. That meant I needed to put his ass in a leg lock or some shit. Just as I sat up about to look for my phone, I heard the shower running.

"Oh." Satisfied that he hadn't left just yet, I lay back down and waited on him to finish.

For the next half hour the water continued to run before it finally stopped. I could hear him fumbling around in his hygiene bag. That was one thing about Brick that was undeniably sexy. He took pride in his appearance and the way he smelled. Seconds later, he walked out dressed in jeans and a tank top. My mouth salivated at his physique. Once he realized my attention was on him, he smiled and licked his lips.

191

"Morning, beautiful. You like what you see?"

"Of course I do."

"Good, I love what I see."

His comment made me blush. "Where are the kids?"

Brick walked over and sat on the edge of the bed. I watched him as he applied lotion to his delicious brown skin. "They was eating breakfast when I got in the shower. They're probably playing the game right now. They was trying to come in and wake you up, but I told them we were gone let you sleep in, since you were tired."

"Well, thank you. I appreciate that."

"That's the best I can do, since you're here the majority of the day with them."

"So, you appreciate me?"

"Of course I do." Brick threw on his shirt and shoes, then he turned to face me. "I'm headed out for a few and no, I won't be gone all day."

I rolled my eyes. "Yeah, right."

"I'm serious, bae."

"We'll see."

Brick leaned down and gave me a pop kiss. "I'm serious. I have a few errands to run and when I get back, we can go to lunch or dinner. Whatever you choose."

"Okay," I tossed the blanket off my body and he walked away. "Well, in the meantime, I'm going by the house and get a few items I left behind."

Brick stopped dead in his tracks at the door and did a full circle in my direction. "No. I'll take you when I get back."

"It won't take that long." I climbed from the bed and headed towards the bathroom.

"How long it'll take isn't the issue. I'm more concerned about you being alone at this point in time, with everything that's going on."

"Baby, relax. It's broad daylight. I'll be okay."

"Did you forget I was shot at in broad daylight?"

There was no point in debating with him, so I threw my hands in the air. "You win."

"Good. Be back soon."

"Oh, and I hope you didn't forget about that Deja situation either. I haven't forgotten about that night."

"Yeah, I know. I heard you in your sleep. I'll handle the bitch, so don't worry about it."

"Oh, I'm not worried. She should be though." That conversation came to a close when he walked out the room and out the door of the hotel room.

"Shit, you taking too long for me," I mumbled and went to take me shower.

Against Brick's wishes, I left the hotel and went by the house anyway. Whenever he conducted business, which was every single day, he lost track of time. I wasn't sweating that though, because he had a family to take care of. As long as he wasn't out dropping dick in a bitch, I couldn't care less about the time he spent getting money. Shit, we had bills and babies to take care of.

Not once did I realize how much I missed being home, until I pulled up in my driveway. This was my safe haven at one point in time, but all of that changed once Brick and I became an item. The moment I changed my life for the better, Daman decided to go ape shit and disturb my peace. I swear that man was so selfish. If only he knew how much I despised him. Sadly, I wished he would've died instead of the guy that was supposed to off him.

"Come on, babies." I removed my seatbelt and got out the car to help them out of the backseat.

As usual, the neighborhood was quiet and to my surprise, I didn't see my neighbor on the porch. He stopped checking on me after his run-in with Brick months ago. After unlocking the door, I stepped to the side and let Legend Jr. and Breanna go inside.

"Sit right there until I come back. I'll be quick." I pointed towards the sofa area.

Once they were seated, I rushed upstairs to grab the things I needed. There were boxes everywhere. "Damn, I'll be glad when we move. I'm tired of living out a damn box and in a hotel."

As I fumbled through the contents of several boxes, my fat ass was out of breath. "Lord, I need some oxygen."

Finally, I came across my favorite lounging dress. Since it had been in a cardboard box since we packed about a week ago, I put it to my nose and inhaled it. Pleased that it still smelled good, I tossed it on the bed and dug through my bins. After spending about fifteen minutes in the room, I had everything I needed, so I tossed it all in my overnight bag and left the room. To my surprise, the kids were mighty quiet.

"They better be sitting down and not all over the place," I mumbled while walking down the steps. "What y'all down here doing?"

When I looked towards the living room, I froze and the bag I was holding slipped from my grip, hitting the floor. My eyes stretched wide in their sockets and my heart skipped several beats. This moment had to be a figment of my imagination, because I just knew wasn't seeing correctly.

"I'm sorry, did I startle you?"

"What the fuck are you doing in my house? And where are my kids?" It was the guy from Brick's apartment that was posing as the backup detective.

"Relax. They're safe." He stood up and stretched. "Too bad I can't say the same for you, since you killed my best friend. Deja isn't too happy about you killing her cousin. So, as you can imagine, this won't end well for you."

The fact he mentioned Deja's name had me furious. I told Brick to handle that bitch, but he was so fucking hardheaded and now this ho' had this nigga here once again. The fool started walking towards me, so I reached down in my purse and pulled out the gun that I took from Brick's apartment. Aimed in his direction and finger on the trigger, I was prepared to shoot.

"Stop right there or I'll shoot you."

With both hands in the air, he smirked. "You don't want to do that."

"I will, so don't try me." He did what I told him not to do and took a step. "I'm warning you. Don't take another step."

Against my wishes, he tried to lunge towards me and that was when I lit his ass up.

Boc! Boc! Boc!

His body jerked as each bullet tore into his chest cavity. Blood splatter flew in every direction, before his body dropped to the floor with a loud thud. From what I could see, he was dead as a doorknob, so I ran outside to find my babies.

Outside, there was a cream van with red letters that read, *Locksmith.* Carefully, I approached the van to make sure no one else was in there. "Bre, LJ., where are you?"

I snatched the passenger door open, but there was no sign of them. Anxiety took over my body and I started to cry. "Oh my God, Brick is going to kill me. He told me not to come here alone."

The guilt made it easy for the tears to fall. If anything happened to the kids, I would never forgive myself for being so careless and hardheaded. Without a doubt, I loved my nephew. He was Legend all over again and having him in my presence filled the void of missing my only brother. Breanna was like a daughter to me and I loved her just as much. If I didn't find them now, I might as well disappear as well.

Quickly, common sense kicked in and I rushed to the back of the van and pulled the door open. Relief consumed me once I saw their faces. Both of them had tape over their mouth.

"Babies I'm so sorry." The van wasn't too high in the air, but I was too big to climb in. "Scoot to me."

Breanna and Legend Jr moved slowly towards me. From the wetness of their faces, they had to have been crying or sweating. That only added insult to injury and I couldn't have that. Not on my watch. When they were close enough, I reached out and pulled them from the van. As soon as I removed the tape from their mouths, the questions came rolling.

"Auntie, who was that man?" Legend asked.

"That's my mama friend," Breanna replied. "I'm telling my daddy on him too. He said we were playing hide and seek, but it was hot in there."

Leaning down, I gave them a hug. "The game is over, okay? I'm going to call your daddy right now. Come on, let's go to the car."

"Auntie, I have to pee." Legend grabbed the front of his pants.

There was no way I could take them back in that house. "Um. Come on, let's go on the side of the house."

"I wanna go in the house," he whined.

"I locked the keys in the house, so we have to wait on your uncle to come."

That was the quickest lie I could come up with, but it worked. Breanna and I had our backs turned, so he could have some privacy. Then, I called Brick.

"What's up, baby?"

"Um. Don't be mad at me please."

Brick took a deep breath. "Zuri, what did you do?"

"We have a problem."

"And, what's that?"

"Okay," I sighed. "Remember you said don't come to the house? Well, I did since I was in the area, and the same thing that happened at your place just occurred again. We're safe though."

"I'm on my way. Sit tight."

"Okay." Brick hung up the phone with the quickness.

A small hand smacked me roughly on my butt. "I'm finished."

Turning on my heels to face him, I smiled. "Okay. Open your hands."

The sanitizer on my key chain came in handy. I squirted a dime-sized amount in his hand. "Rub your hands together." When he was done, we walked to my car and got inside to wait on Brick.

Chapter 20
Zuri

The sound of tires screeching pulled my attention towards the road. When I looked back, I could see Brick's car zooming up the driveway right before he slammed on brakes. He jumped out the car and ran towards us. Coop jumped out from the passenger side and leaned against the car. That didn't come as a surprise, because I knew he wouldn't be too far behind.

Brick opened up the passenger door in the back and peeked in. "Y'all okay?"

Both kids nodded their heads. His attention was immediately placed on me. "Get out the car," he demanded.

Oh shit! I thought, before opening up the car door and climbing out. Brick pushed the door closed and looked me in the eyes. "Bruh, you don't listen for shit. I specifically told yo' ass don't come here. You don't listen for shit."

"Well, I needed to get my stuff and I knew you were going to take all day. We were close by the neighborhood, so I stopped. Damn, I'm sorry."

Brick sighed, then rubbed his face in aggravation. Since he had an attitude, I caught one just as big.

"If you handled that bitch like I told you to, none of this would've happened." Now, I was fuming with my hand on my hips. "You act like you can't do it or some shit. What, you still got feelings for that bitch?"

"Man, chill out, 'cause you know the answer to that dumb ass question. I told you I'm gon' handle her. Just chill and tell me what happened."

"The same guy from the house showed up again and said Deja sent him." Now, he was standing there, looking stupid. "Nah, don't get quiet now. You was ready to curse me out when you thought it was one of Daman's friends."

"Take the kids back to the room and I'll be there after we clean this shit up."

Brick tried walking off, but I grabbed his arm. "Are you gone handle this or what? This the second time this ho' came for me and I'm not letting it slide."

He snatched his arm from my grip and looked past me. "Come on, Coop."

"So, you gone ignore me?"

Brick had me so livid, I could no longer contain my anger. He was acting as if it was my fault. Since he wanted to act like I did something wrong, I gave him a reason to be mad. Using all of my strength, I balled up my fist and decked him in the face.

"What the fuck wrong with you?" Brick stepped so close to me, I could feel the air coming from his nostrils.

"You are what's wrong with me. Last night you promised to protect me and you failed. You fucking failed," I screamed. "You keep letting this ho' send people to harm me and your fucking child."

Coop ran over and stood in the middle of us. He placed his hand on Brick's chest. "Bruh, don't do it. This yo' lady and she pregnant. Let her blow off some steam."

He stood there taking short quick breaths, while mean mugging me. "I'm good. I ain't gone hit her, bruh."

"Excuse me." I pushed Coop's arm out the way and grabbed the handle of my car door. Before I opened it, I wiped the tears from my eyes and looked back at Brick. "You don't love me and you probably never did. Fuck you and this engagement."

That was all I needed to say before I snatched the door open. Suddenly, I felt a hand grip my arm. "Zuri, wait."

"No!" I shouted. "Let me go."

Coop jumped in. "Bruh, let her cool off."

"Listen to your homeboy." I jumped in the car and peeled out the driveway, burning rubber.

Going to the hotel was the last thing I wanted to do, so I rode around for a good thirty minutes before I came up with a plan. When I made it to a red light, I fumbled through my purse and took out my cellphone to call Shakira. It was time for Legend to go back with his mother. Shit was about to get real crazy and I couldn't have him in the mix, so I dialed her number.

"The number you have reached is no longer in service."

I looked down at my phone. "What?"

That had me blown, so I dialed her number two more times and it said the same thing. "Relax, Z. Maybe she forgot to pay her phone bill. Just call her on Messenger."

The light changed and I pulled off. Quickly, I opened up the Facebook app and searched for her name. Nothing. That was weird to me, but I had important business to handle. Instead of going to the hotel I called Mehzani.

"Hey, sis."

"Zani, do me a favor and go on your Facebook and see if you can find Shakira's profile for me please."

"Okay, hold up. I'm putting you on speaker."

"Okay."

Periodically, I would look back and check on the kids. They hadn't said a word since we were at the house. Brick and I did our best to not argue in front of Breanna, but today I lost it.

"I don't see her page anymore. She probably deactivated that and her Instagram."

"Girl, I have L.J. and her phone disconnected. She asked me to keep him for a few days, but that was a little over a week ago."

"Damn, sis. It sounds like she hit it on you."

"You think so?"

"Hell, yeah. Why else would she disappear and," Mehzani paused. "Wait—"

"What happened?"

"Now that I think about it, she made a post the other day about Legend. She mentioned something about being with him again and that she couldn't live without him."

"Damn." That news blew the fuck out of me, but right now, I couldn't focus on that. "Aye, can you watch the kids for a few hours for me please? I'll pay you."

"Nah, you good, sis. Just bring them over."

"You're a life saver. I'm on my way."

"Okay see you in a few."
"Alright."

***

By the time I took the kids to get food, dropped them off to Mehzani and went to Walmart, it was dark as hell outside. The clock on my dash said it was going on eleven o'clock. That was perfect timing for me. The neighborhood was quiet and no one was outside. As I proceeded with caution, I killed the lights and backed into the driveway. Checking my surroundings once more, I slid on the ski mask and grabbed my gun, before making my way to the front door. Just as I was about to knock on the door, I could hear the locks disengaging, so I stepped to the side. The second I saw the first foot step onto the porch, I bum rushed the bitch, while jamming my gun in her stomach.

"Back the fuck up, ho'."

Deja held her hands at her side and backed up into the house. I followed suit and kicked the door closed.

"I don't have money if that's what you looking for. Just lease don't hurt me. I have kids."

"That's funny, coming from a dog-ass ho' that don't give two fucks about her daughter's safety."

Deja's brow bent and she tilted her head to the side. "What are you talking about?"

"Now you wanna play dumb and I ain't on that shit. You know what the fuck you did." Removing the ski mask, I revealed my face. "Remember what you did now?"

Deja sat down on the sofa, but she never took her eyes off of me or my weapon. "Did Brick send you here?"

"You don't get to ask questions, bitch. Why the fuck did you send your cousin to cause harm to me and my kids?"

"Your kids?" she repeated. "Breanna is not your child."

"Could've fooled me." I held up my hand and flashed my ring finger at her. "Brick feels otherwise."

"Bitch, fuck you, Brick and that ring." That was her first mistake, calling me out my name. She needed to show me some respect, so I popped her ass dead in the mouth.

Whap!

"Watch your mouth, 'cause I've had enough of your shit. You haven't even tried to see your child. I guess you too busy getting fucked. So, it seems to me having a wet ass is more important to you than being a mother."

"You happy you having his baby. Newsflash, you ain't the only one to have a baby by him and keep thinking he gone marry you, fool," Deja laughed sinisterly.

"Oh, we are getting married, but too bad you won't be alive to witness it. No worries, though. I will take care of Breanna the same way I do now. Except, I will be her legal guardian and mother once this adoption goes through."

That wiped the stupid grin off her face. "I'm not worried about you killing me. That's not in you, and what adoption papers? I didn't give him my daughter."

"That's not your business." I pointed the gun at her. "So, is there anything you wish to tell her before you leave this world?"

"You're not gonna get away with this. And, if you kill me, who do you think is going to raise your child?"

"The same person that's raising yours now, dummy. Me. Fuck you thought?"

"Yeah whatever. You keep thinking that." Deja leaned back on the sofa and folded her arms.

"You really don't believe I will shoot you, huh?" Apparently, no one told the dumb ho' I was responsible for killing her cousin. "Well, I guess I should fill you in a little secret. I'm the one that killed your cousin."

Deja's eyes expanded and her jaw hit the floor. "What?"

"Don't get scared now. I'm the one that killed your cousin." I made my way over to where she was sitting and slapped the shit out of her. She grabbed her face, but didn't utter a word.

"What type of mother could put their child in danger, just to get back at the father? You have to be a special kind of stupid to do some shit like that."

The vibration of my cellphone silenced the remainder of my words. So, I pulled it from my pocket and checked the screen. It was Brick's stank ass. We had nothing to discuss at this point. Every word I'd said, I meant and he wasn't changing my mind about it.

"Fuck you," I mumbled and tucked my phone away quickly. Deja was rocking back and forth on the sofa, with her hand behind her back. "What the fuck you doing?"

"Nothing."

"Get up right now." The sudden change in her demeanor told me something was up. My phone went off again and it was Brick calling. "Stop fucking calling me."

The bitch was taking too long to get up, so I snatched her up by her hair. An object hit the floor with a loud thump and when I looked down, I realized it was a cellphone.

"Who the fuck did you call?" If she was able to call the police, my ass was in a world of trouble.

The suspense was driving me crazy, so I bent down and snatched up the phone. When I checked the call log, I saw two outgoing calls to Brick's phone. "What the fuck you calling him for?"

Deja fixed her lips to say something, but before she could get it out, I backhanded her. "You stupid bitch. He can't save you."

The impact of the slap caused her to stumble, so I grabbed her by the hair and dragged her outside. "I'ma teach you, ho', about playing with me and my damn baby."

"Let go of my hair," she whined, as she tried her damnedest to keep up with my fast footwork.

There was nothing she could say to me that would stop me from doing her ass in. Once I made it to the trunk, I popped the lock on it and raised the trunk.

"Get in."

"Nooo!" She shook her head repeatedly and sobbed. "Please, just let me go. I'm sorry. I should've never done that. Just understand where I'm coming from."

"I didn't ask for any last words. I gave you a command, so you need to follow it."

"Forgive me for the sake of my children," Deja begged, with her hands folded like she was praying.

"Get your ass in the trunk because you pissing me off. You wasn't worried about your kids when you was fucking Gucci, who happens to be my sister's boyfriend, by the way."

The look on her face said she was stunned.

"Don't look surprised. I know all about it." With a lot of force, I pushed her into the trunk.

Her body collided against the car hard. "Fuck!" she screeched.

More force was needed, because I had a feeling Brick was headed this way. So, I pushed her again, causing her to fall inside. Satisfied, I attempted to close the trunk. "Nooo!" Deja shouted and kicked me in the stomach. My reflexes and motherly instincts caused me to pull the trigger with no hesitation.

Boca!

Chapter 21

Brick

"Bruh, I got it from here. You can go check on your lady. If you don't, you might lose her." Coop looked at me with sympathy in his eyes.

"She ain't going nowhere." That was a fact and I was confident with my answer.

"You sure about that?"

"One thing I know is that Zuri is big on family. She don't want to be a single mother."

"I get that, but I understand why she mad. Deja been coming for you hard and you haven't responded to her yet. I'm yo' nigga and you ain't told me shit, so I'm confused too."

All of that made sense, but I had to move in silence. I didn't expect Zuri to feel where I was coming from, but I expected Coop to catch my drift.

"You know me better than my lady, and you know I don't play about my daughter, period. Deja could've gotten my daughter killed on three separate occasions, so her days on earth are limited. Moving with caution is my biggest thing, especially since I filed for full custody."

I tapped Coop on his shoulder with my hand. "Who is going to be the first suspect if she comes up missing? Me." I hit my chest. "I can't go to prison for killing her. My daughter needs me more than anything."

"Okay." He nodded. "I feel you on that."

"I been had a plan for her, but I have to do it at the right time and it has to be perfect. No one cares if you kill a drug dealer, but if you kill a woman, a mother at that, the media will eat this up. The detectives on the case will work hard for answers and I can't afford to have that type of heat on me."

"That makes sense." Coop agreed with a head nod.

"Zuri has to be patient."

"Explain that to her, so she will know you have every intention of handling that."

"I've been trying to call her, but she not answering. Then, Deja been calling, but she ain't getting nothing but the voicemail. That ho' can't say shit to me, real spill."

"Fuck her, 'cause she tried it and deserves everything that's coming her way."

My cellphone started ringing and vibrating hard on the coffee table. So, I walked over to retrieve it. Flashing across the screen was Janae's name. Normally, she wouldn't call me this late, unless she needed a ride from work. Now, she had a car, so that couldn't be it. I picked it up.

"What's up, Nae?"

"Daddy, I need you," she cried. "Please."

The sound of her voice sent me into panic mode. If I had to fuck somebody up about my goddaughter, it was going down. "Janae, what's wrong, baby?"

"I'm in the hospital and I need you up here now."

"What happened to you?"

"Just come to Florida Medical Center. I'm in room fifty-one-fifty."

"I'm on my way."

"Okay."

When I hung up the phone, I could feel an instant headache coming on. I didn't know what I was about to run up on, but I was praying it wasn't too bad. However, based on the fact that she was talking to me, it told me shit wasn't that bad. At least, I hoped that's what that meant.

"What's up with Nae, bruh?"

"Ion know." I rubbed my temple with my fingers. "She said she in the hospital and she need me to come up there now."

"Well, what you waiting on? Go and check on her. I got this here. Just keep me posted, while I go drop this body in the lake."

"A'ight." Standing on my feet, Coop and I G-hugged. "I'll hit you up later."

"Fa'sho."

Florida Medical Center was only a fifteen-minute drive from Zuri's house, but I cut that time down the middle. The urgency in her voice kept playing in my head, fucking with my mind. My prayers for her were on repeat. I made it to the fifth floor and that was when I noticed Janae standing in the hallway. Demarcus was holding her in his arms when I approached them.

"Nae, baby," I rubbed her back. "What's going on, Demarcus?"

"Sup Brick." He released her from his grip. "I'll let her tell you."

Janae turned around and wrapped her arms around me. "It's my mama, Brick. It's bad."

"Where is she?"

"In the room."

"Come on."

We walked inside the room and I froze when I saw Shan hooked up to a machine and several cords coming from her body. Immediately, I rushed to her bedside and rubbed her hair.

"Shan, I'm here."

The strong woman I saw not too long ago, was now weak and frail. It seemed as if she was malnourished by her weight loss. Shan's eyes fluttered before she opened them completely. A faint smile spread across her lips.

"You came."

"Of course I did." Slowly, she raised her hand and touched mine. It was cool to the touch, but I held hers in mine. "You know I'll always come to you. What's going on with you?"

"The cancer has become aggressive and there's nothing else they can do for me."

A lone tear slipped from my eye and down my cheek. To see her suffer was weighing down on me hard, and I couldn't help but to feel bad for the terrible hand she had been dealt. Shan saw me cry before, so I didn't feel embarrassed.

"No. I'm not going for that. I'll have you moved to a better hospital, so you can get the best treatment possible. I'll pay for everything."

Shan's lips were dry like she was dehydrated and her face was a lot smaller than normal. Although she was sick, she was still trying to remain in good spirits, as she forced a smile. "That's just like Brick. Always wanting to fix things." She placed her other hand on top of mine and rubbed it. "That's what I always loved about you."

"That wouldn't be me if I didn't try to fix things." As I wiped my eyes, I mustered up a smile. "I'm Superman, remember?"

"Yes I remember calling you that all the time." Shan moved one of her hands and placed it on her stomach. "You know, I never stopped loving you."

We had a good relationship, so I could definitely believe that without a doubt. "I love you too."

"No. You don't get it. I've loved you since we were younger and I've been in love with you ever since. When things didn't work out between us, I was hurt. All I wanted was to be with you and only you, but you didn't feel that way about me."

The emotions she was displaying took me back to our younger days and I knew I did her wrong. She had a gangsta about to break down in that bitch.

"It's not that I didn't want the same thing, I was young. I didn't know anything about being in love, or loving a young lady at that time. Charge it to my head and not my heart."

"I forgave you a long time ago."

"Thank you. I appreciate that."

"You're welcome."

"How can I make it up to you? Because you are getting out of this hospital." I tried to lighten the mood. Truth be told, I wasn't ready to part ways with Shan and I knew with the proper treatment, she would be okay.

Shan closed her eyes, took a deep breath and release the air slowly. "Brick, I am going to die. I know you don't want to accept that, but you have to. I've made peace with myself and

God, and I'm prepared to go into my next phase of life, whatever that might be. There is one thing I need from you."

"Whatever it is, I'll do it."

Silence took over the room for a few seconds, but Janae walked in, talking to Demarcus. "Janae," Shan's voice was hoarse.

"Yes, Mommy?" Her eyes were bloodshot red when she walked up to the bed and held her mother's hand.

"I love you so much."

"I love you too."

"And I'm so sorry I'm not going to be here to see you go off to college." As Shan continued to talk, we were all in heavy tears, including Nae's boyfriend. I continued to hold her hand.

"When I gave birth to you, I promised myself I was going to be the best mother I could be. I always had plans for you to go to college and become a better woman than I am."

"You're a great mother and this is not your fault." Janae sniffled. "I promise to make you proud of me."

"I'm already proud of you, so don't ever doubt that. You've been the perfect daughter."

Shan closed her eyes and looked away. "I just wish I made better choices when it came down to your father. I'm the reason he was missing from your life like that. You could've had so much more if it wasn't for me being so young, dumb and selfish. I hope you can forgive me."

"I'm not upset and it's not your fault he's in prison. Brick has been a good daddy to me, so I'm not missing anything." Janae stepped up and hugged her mother tight. "I never missed a beat in life and that was because of you. I don't know what I'm going to do without you. Why do you have to leave me so soon? I'm not ready, Mommy. My heart can't take this pain."

Janae screamed and made everyone jump. That was my cue to get up and comfort her. Demarcus stood up, but I signaled him to stay seated. The grip she had on Shan was tight as hell, but I managed to pull her away and embrace her.

"Nae, I promise I'll be here for you. I will never leave your side. I will be there to see you graduate from college. I'm going to walk you down the aisle and be in the delivery room when you have kids. This is going to be hard for both of us, but we will get through this together."

"This is not fair. Life is not fair. Why do I have to lose my mother?" she screamed repeatedly.

"Janae? Baby, calm down, please," Shan pleaded.

For the next few minutes, I spent my time consoling her and getting my baby to relax. I knew she was going to need me more than ever.

The monitor Shan was hooked to started to make a loud beeping noise, sending our nerves in a frenzy. Janae and I attended to her mother. Seconds later, the nurse came rushing through the door and to the bed. We stood back and watched her check Shan's vital signs. Silently, I was praying she was going to be okay. This couldn't be her last day on earth.

After the nurse was done, the monitor was back to making its regular noise and we were relieved. The nurse looked at us with a great deal of concern. "Her blood pressure has gone up drastically and her heart is beating irregularly, but she's okay right now."

"Thanks," I replied.

Once the nurse left, we went back to the bed with Shan. It seemed like she was tired and ready to give up on life. That didn't sit well with me, and I was going to talk to her about going to another hospital. Now wasn't the time, so I put it in the back of my mind for the next day.

"I need you two to listen to what I'm about to say." Shan looked me and Janae in the eyes. "Brick, I appreciate everything you've done for us over the years, and I know you will keep your word. Please take care of my baby girl."

"I got her, Shan. I promise."

"There is something I need to say before this monitor goes off and I die for real this time."

Whenever I left the hospital, I knew I was going to need a stiff drink and a shoulder to cry on. Never in life did I think I would be saying goodbye to my first love.

"My intentions were always good with you, Brick, and you know I loved you to death. You were my first and I wished you were my only, but life had other plans for us. Janae, you are the air that I breathe and always remember I never meant to hurt you."

"Hurt me how?" Janae asked.

Shan wiped her falling tears and looked me in the eyes. "Janae is your daughter."

"Huh?" My ears couldn't believe what they were hearing and apparently, Janae couldn't either because her mouth was wide open. "My daughter?" I repeated. "Are you sure?"

"Yes. Do you remember the very last time I saw you and we had sex?"

I nodded my head.

"A few weeks later, I found out I was pregnant. I didn't have the guts to tell you the truth, so I slept with him to cover it up. I did that so you wouldn't ask questions. I'm sorry y'all. Don't hate me."

Janae walked away and sat next to Demarcus.

"Shan, I don't hate you, but why didn't you tell me this years ago? You know I would've taken care of my responsibilities."

"You wasn't ready to be a father, because you wasn't ready to be in a relationship. I knew how that was going to turn out, so I kept it a secret." Shan shook her head from side to side. "I'm sorry for disrupting your life with this, and I hope this doesn't ruin your relationship. For Janae's sake, I couldn't go to the grave with this secret. All I ask is that you don't hate me."

The secret she laid out on the table like a Sunday dinner was enough to feed a thousand men. It was certainly a lot to take in and I needed to sit down. So, I lay down in the bed with Shan and held her in my arms.

"I'm not mad at you and I don't hate you. Back then, I was wild and I could see how my reckless behavior drove you to think

211

I wasn't ready. My only problem is, why didn't you tell me sooner? I've been here all her life and I feel like that was something I needed to know."

"I been wanted to tell you, but every time I got close to saying those words, I lost my nerve. If you want to take a DNA test to confirm, you can do so. But, I know without a doubt, that you're her father and I'm sorry for not telling you sooner."

Shan's words were sincere and I knew it came from the heart. We stared in each other's eyes and I kissed her gently. "Shan, I love you and I always will. You have my word that I will take care of our daughter. People make mistakes and we were kids. Don't worry about my relationship, I'll handle that. Even if she doesn't accept it, which I highly doubt, because she's not like that at all, I will never abandon her. You have no worries. I'm going to take care of her the same way I take care of Breanna."

"Thank you," she whispered.

"You don't have to thank me. She's my responsibility now."

As I held Shan in my arms, I didn't want to imagine life without her. My words were sincere also, because I still loved her. I just knew we could never be together. The friend zone seemed like it was better for us, so we didn't cross that line. The sound of the monitor beeped long and hard once again, interrupting my stroll down memory lane. When I looked at Shan, her eyes were closed. Placing my hand over her heart, I realized it was no longer beating and in that moment, mine stopped too, temporarily. Tears streamed down my face and my heart broke in a million pieces, as I kissed her forehead.

"I love you, Shan. Sleep in peace, my angel."

"Nooo!" Janae screamed and rushed over to me. I jumped from the bed and took her into my arms. "I want my mommy back."

"Nae, baby, it's going to be okay. Daddy will be here for you as long as I have breath in my body."

I was fine with Janae being my daughter. However, Zuri was another story. I wasn't sure how she was going to take the news, but it wouldn't be long before she found out.

To Be Continued...
Corrupted by a Gangsta 4
Coming Soon

Submission Guideline

Submit the first three chapters of your completed manuscript to ldpsubmissions@gmail.com, subject line: Your book's title. The manuscript must be in a .doc file and sent as an attachment. Document should be in Times New Roman, double spaced and in size 12 font. Also, provide your synopsis and full contact information. If sending multiple submissions, they must each be in a separate email.

Have a story but no way to send it electronically? You can still submit to LDP/Ca$h Presents. Send in the first three chapters, written or typed, of your completed manuscript to:

LDP: Submissions Dept
Po Box 870494
Mesquite, Tx 75187

DO NOT send original manuscript. Must be a duplicate.

Provide your synopsis and a cover letter containing your full contact information.

Thanks for considering LDP and Ca$h Presents.

Coming Soon from Lock Down Publications/Ca$h Presents

BOW DOWN TO MY GANGSTA

By **Ca$h**

TORN BETWEEN TWO

By **Coffee**

BLOOD STAINS OF A SHOTTA **III**

By **Jamaica**

STEADY MOBBIN **III**

By **Marcellus Allen**

BLOOD OF A BOSS **V**

By **Askari**

LOYAL TO THE GAME **IV**

LIFE OF SIN

By **T.J. & Jelissa**

A DOPEBOY'S PRAYER **II**

By **Eddie "Wolf" Lee**

IF LOVING YOU IS WRONG… **III**

LOVE ME EVEN WHEN IT HURTS **II**

By **Jelissa**

TRUE SAVAGE **VI**

By **Chris Green**

BLAST FOR ME **III**

A BRONX TALE

By **Ghost**

ADDICTIED TO THE DRAMA **III**

By **Jamila Mathis**

LIPSTICK KILLAH **III**

CRIME OF PASSION **II**

By **Mimi**

WHAT BAD BITCHES DO **III**

KILL ZONE **II**

By **Aryanna**

THE COST OF LOYALTY **II**

By **Kweli**

SHE FELL IN LOVE WITH A REAL ONE **II**

By **Tamara Butler**

LOVE SHOULDN'T HURT **III**

RENEGADE BOYS **II**

By **Meesha**

CORRUPTED BY A GANGSTA **IV**

By **Destiny Skai**

A GANGSTER'S CODE **III**

By **J-Blunt**

KING OF NEW YORK III

By **T.J. Edwards**

CUM FOR ME **IV**

By **Ca$h & Company**

GORILLAS IN THE BAY

De'Kari

THE STREETS ARE CALLING

Duquie Wilson

KINGPIN KILLAZ II

Hood Rich

STEADY MOBBIN' **III**

Marcellus Allen

SINS OF A HUSTLER

ASAD

HER MAN, MINE'S TOO **II**

Nicole Goosby

GORILLAZ IN THE BAY **II**

DE'KARI

TRIGGADALE II

Elijah R. Freeman

THE STREETS ARE CALLING **II**

Duquie Wilson

Available Now

RESTRAINING ORDER **I & II**

By **CA$H & Coffee**

LOVE KNOWS NO BOUNDARIES **I II & III**

By **Coffee**

RAISED AS A GOON I, II, III & IV

BRED BY THE SLUMS I, II, III

BLAST FOR ME I & II

ROTTEN TO THE CORE I III

By **Ghost**

LAY IT DOWN **I & II**

LAST OF A DYING BREED

BLOOD STAINS OF A SHOTTA I & II

By **Jamaica**

LOYAL TO THE GAME

LOYAL TO THE GAME II

LOYAL TO THE GAME III

By **TJ & Jelissa**

BLOODY COMMAS I & II

SKI MASK CARTEL I II & III

KING OF NEW YORK I II

By **T.J. Edwards**

IF LOVING HIM IS WRONG…I & II

LOVE ME EVEN WHEN IT HURTS

By **Jelissa**

WHEN THE STREETS CLAP BACK I & II III

By **Jibril Williams**

A DISTINGUISHED THUG STOLE MY HEART I II & III

LOVE SHOULDN'T HURT I II

RENEGADE BOYS

By **Meesha**

A GANGSTER'S CODE I & II

By J-Blunt

PUSH IT TO THE LIMIT

By **Bre' Hayes**

BLOOD OF A BOSS **I, II, III & IV**

By **Askari**

THE STREETS BLEED MURDER **I, II & III**

THE HEART OF A GANGSTA I II& III

By **Jerry Jackson**

CUM FOR ME

CUM FOR ME 2

CUM FOR ME 3

An **LDP Erotica Collaboration**

BRIDE OF A HUSTLA **I II & II**

THE FETTI GIRLS **I, II& III**

CORRUPTED BY A GANGSTA I, II & III

By **Destiny Skai**

WHEN A GOOD GIRL GOES BAD

By **Adrienne**

A GANGSTER'S REVENGE **I II III & IV**

THE BOSS MAN'S DAUGHTERS

THE BOSS MAN'S DAUGHTERS II

THE BOSSMAN'S DAUGHTERS III

THE BOSSMAN'S DAUGHTERS IV

THE BOSS MAN'S DAUGHTERS **V**

A SAVAGE LOVE **I & II**

BAE BELONGS TO ME

A HUSTLER'S DECEIT I, II

WHAT BAD BITCHES DO I, II

By **Aryanna**

A KINGPIN'S AMBITON

A KINGPIN'S AMBITION **II**

I MURDER FOR THE DOUGH

By **Ambitious**

TRUE SAVAGE

TRUE SAVAGE II

TRUE SAVAGE **III**

TRUE SAVAGE **IV**

TRUE SAVAGE **V**

By **Chris Green**

A DOPEBOY'S PRAYER

By **Eddie "Wolf" Lee**

THE KING CARTEL **I, II & III**

By **Frank Gresham**

THESE NIGGAS AIN'T LOYAL **I, II & III**

By **Nikki Tee**

GANGSTA SHYT **I II &III**

By **CATO**

THE ULTIMATE BETRAYAL

By **Phoenix**

BOSS'N UP **I , II & III**

By **Royal Nicole**

I LOVE YOU TO DEATH

By Destiny J

I RIDE FOR MY HITTA

I STILL RIDE FOR MY HITTA

By **Misty Holt**

LOVE & CHASIN' PAPER

By **Qay Crockett**

TO DIE IN VAIN

By **ASAD**

BROOKLYN HUSTLAZ

By **Boogsy Morina**

BROOKLYN ON LOCK I & II

By **Sonovia**

GANGSTA CITY

By **Teddy Duke**

A DRUG KING AND HIS DIAMOND I & II III

A DOPEMAN'S RICHES

HER MAN, MINE'S TOO

By Nicole Goosby

TRAPHOUSE KING **I II & III**

KINGPIN KILLAZ

By **Hood Rich**

LIPSTICK KILLAH **I, II**

CRIME OF PASSION

By **Mimi**

STEADY MOBBN' **I, II**

By **Marcellus Allen**

WHO SHOT YA **I, II**

Renta

GORILLAZ IN THE BAY

DE'KARI

TRIGGADALE

Elijah R. Freeman

GOD BLESS THE TRAPPERS I, II, III

THESE SCANDALOUS STREETS I, II, III

FEAR MY GANGSTA I, II

THESE STREETS DON'T LOVE NOBODY I, II

Tranay Adams

THE STREETS ARE CALLING

Duquie Wilson

BOOKS BY LDP'S CEO, CA$H

TRUST IN NO MAN

TRUST IN NO MAN 2

TRUST IN NO MAN 3

BONDED BY BLOOD

SHORTY GOT A THUG

THUGS CRY

THUGS CRY 2

THUGS CRY 3

TRUST NO BITCH

TRUST NO BITCH 2

TRUST NO BITCH 3

TIL MY CASKET DROPS

RESTRAINING ORDER

RESTRAINING ORDER 2

IN LOVE WITH A CONVICT

Coming Soon

BONDED BY BLOOD 2

BOW DOWN TO MY GANGSTA